"TELL ME WHEN TO STOP . . ."

Jeremy imprisoned Anne in a strong embrace and kissed her cheeks, eyelids and the hollow of her neck. She shuddered with pleasure as he lowered her onto a bed of soft leaves. Her blood seemed on fire as it coursed through her veins. Her heart pounded as if it were threatening to escape from her chest and fly away. Anne returned Jeremy's kisses with abandon, her body tingling with almost unbearable pleasure when he slowly unbuttoned her shirt.

"Shall I stop?" he teased. . . .

ELEANOR FROST lives in Ohio, where she is the society editor of a small-town daily newspaper. She began her career in journalism as the staff photographer for a service newspaper at the Naval Air Station, Pensacola, Florida. She enjoys reading, sewing, and, of course, writing.

Dear Reader:

The editors of Rapture Romance have only one thing to say—thank you! Your response to our authors, both the newcomers and the established favorites, has been enthusiastic and loyal, and we, who love our books, appreciate it.

We are committed to bringing you romances after your own heart, with the tender sensuality you've asked for and the quality you deserve. We hope that you will continue to enjoy our Rapture Romances each month as much as we enjoy bringing them to you.

To tell you about upcoming books, introduce you to the authors, and give you an inside look at the world of Rapture Romance, we have started a free monthly newsletter. Just write to *The Rapture Reader* at the address shown below, and we will be happy to send you each issue.

And please keep writing to us! Your comments and letters have already helped us to bring you better and better books—the kind *you* want—and we depend on them. Of course, our authors also eagerly await your letters. While we can't give out their addresses, we are happy to forward any mail—writers need to hear from their fans!

Happy reading!

The Editors
Rapture Romance
New American Library
1633 Broadway
New York, NY 10019

ELUSIVE PARADISE

by

Eleanor Frost

RAPTURE ROMANCE

NEW AMERICAN LIBRARY

PUBLISHER'S NOTE

This novel is a work of fiction. Names, characters, places, and incidents either are the product of the author's imagination or are used fictitiously, and any resemblance to actual persons, living or dead, events, or locales is entirely coincidental.

Copyright © 1984 by Eleanor Frost

SIGNET, SIGNET CLASSIC, MENTOR, PLUME, MERIDIAN AND NAL BOOKS
are published by The New American Library, Inc.,
1633 Broadway, New York, New York 10019

First Printing, February, 1984

1 2 3 4 5 6 7 8 9

PRINTED IN THE UNITED STATES OF AMERICA

*To Lois Walker, Joe Gilmore,
and Evelyn Frohman, all of whom
played important parts
in making this book possible*

Chapter One

Anne would have accepted any interruption that took her away from the work she was doing in the ledger, but the interruption that came turned out to be exceptional.

She was trying to estimate her expenses for the winter months, when her small crafts shop would be closed. No matter how miserly she tried to be as she added up her food, utility, and car costs for the winter, the figure came out to be more than her bank balance. The tourist season was over in this small northern Michigan resort town, and she couldn't count on any more income until spring. The all-too-abundant red ink in her ledger only confirmed what the loan officer at the Bank of Paradise had said when he turned down her small-business loan the previous spring.

"A lot of you city people come to Paradise and think you can have an easy, stress-free existence running some kind of small business up here, Miss Keene. The Upper Peninsula of Michigan isn't a rest home for burned-out city dwellers. Businesses succeed or fail in Paradise on the same principles that they do in the big cities, with the added disadvantage that you can do business only during the tourist season, and that is only six months a year. Pie-in-the-sky dreams of a 'cute little shop' aren't enough. I'm sorry to have to say it, but I doubt you'll last out the first winter."

He hadn't sounded sorry at all, and Anne determined to prove him wrong. She opened her shop without the extra capital the loan would have provided.

But April's enthusiasm was turning into October's despair. Her summer profits had barely kept her going, and now, with six months until she could count on another customer, she knew that she had failed. Anne's eyes went back to the top of the column of figures and ran down it again. There had to be something she could eliminate, something she could do without that would make her meager funds stretch until April. There wasn't. A single lamp burned at her desk. She never turned on more than one light at a time, and the tiniest of fires burned in her wood stove. The wood was free, cut on the property she'd purchased with the shop, but since she had to pay a man to cut it, she was determined to make this cord last as long as possible. The tires on her ancient Volkswagen Bug were practically bald, and she knew she had to have snow tires before the winter set in. There wasn't anything she could do.

Even as she forced herself to concentrate on her financial predicament, Anne was secretly praying for something to come and take her away from the unhappy facts in her ledger.

Her prayers were answered when a strong knock came on her door. Anne pushed herself away from the antique rolltop desk and crossed the dark salesroom. She cautiously opened the door just a crack and peeked out into the night.

"I'm sorry, but we're closed," she said to the tall, dark shape of a man who stood outside. City-bred, she would never simply open her door to a stranger this late at night.

The stranger took the matter out of her hands. He pushed the door back firmly and stepped inside. Anne fairly jumped back from the door.

"I beg your pardon," she sputtered.

"I'm sorry," the man said. In the dark room Anne still couldn't tell much about his looks. "But I'm not interested in buying souvenirs. My car broke down and I need to use your phone. Where is it?" His tone was firm and supremely confident.

"I'm sorry, too. I don't have a phone."

In the dim light Anne thought she saw a look of annoyance pass across his shadowy features.

"Excuse me," she said sarcastically. "If I'd known that you were coming, I would have had one installed."

"If you live here alone, you really ought to have a phone," he said in an infuriating, take-charge manner. "If you had any trouble, how would you call for help? It's at least two miles to your nearest neighbor."

"What *is* this?" Anne snapped. "Are you from the phone company? What do you mean pushing your way into my home in the middle of the night to tell me that I need a phone? Are you crazy?"

The man, whoever he was, laughed. He laughed the way people laugh when they're at the end of their rope and they finally see the absurdity of their situation.

"I'm sorry, really sorry. I didn't mean to be so rude," he said in an entirely different tone. All the command was gone now. "I've driven all the way from Chicago, and it's been a very long day."

"Two miles? There's nothing within two miles of here," Anne replied, remembering his comment about the distance to her nearest neighbor. "My nearest neighbor is John Blackbear, four miles back. You must be lost as well."

"Ah, let me correct you. Better yet, let me introduce myself. I'm Jeremy Breck. I'm moving into the old Breck place, two miles up the road."

"That old wreck of a house up on the hill?"

"Well, I know that nobody has lived up there since

my grandfather died, fifteen years ago, but the house is basically sound and I intend to fix it up."

"You'd better be one awfully good fixer, but never mind that now. I'm afraid that the best help I can offer you is a ride to the motel back in Paradise. Mort's Garage will be closed at this time of night, so I doubt that you can get a tow until morning." Anne wondered at her courage, offering a strange man a ride, but his change in attitude had warmed her. Something told her that she was going to like this man, even if she couldn't see what he looked like.

"Do you have a flashlight? Maybe if I could see what I was doing, I could fix it."

"A flashlight I have. Just a minute and I'll get it." Anne reached over to the wall and flipped on the lights. The little shop sprang to life in a blaze of glittering color. Anne had a wide variety of consignment crafts and needlework on display, but the most prominent pieces were her own stained-glass works. Most were suspended from the rafters by nearly invisible monofilament threads. There were window panels, smaller sun catchers for hanging in windows, and elaborate, jewellike mobiles.

A stained-glass parrot perched in a bamboo ring; a common enough object, but in Anne's version of the bird, the wings were spread and one foot was drawn up—the figure was seemingly caught in the act of taking off from its perch. The bird, resplendent in its ruby-and-emerald plumes, hung just a few inches from Jeremy's head, and the bright flash of color from the bird as the lights came on drew his eyes to it. Anne had a brief moment to observe him before he turned his attention back to her.

He had curly, unruly, but not unkempt dark hair. His eyebrows rose in high, expressive arches over deep, dark brown eyes that were rimmed with a thick finge of dark lashes. His cheeks were sharply sculpted, showing the evening shadow of a heavy beard. The aquiline nose pointed to a rakish, dark mustache above a wide, humorous mouth. His jawline was firm, accented by an impish dimple in the middle of his chin. Anne's first impression was of a television private detective whose name she couldn't remember. It had been ages since she'd watched television.

He was wearing a red-and-black–plaid flannel shirt over a dark turtleneck sweater. His shoulders were broad, his waist was narrow, and his faded jeans fit his thick, muscular thighs perfectly.

"Flashlight," he reminded her as he noticed Anne's stare.

"Yes, flashlight," Anne replied dumbly, embarrassed to have been caught staring.

She pulled an electric lantern out from under the counter. Jeremy's eyes never left her and she was anxious to move into the dark, where she wouldn't be under his appraising eye. She knew that her looks were nothing to be ashamed of, but she had hardly been prepared to receive visitors. Her shoulder-length, wheat-blond hair was pulled into two convenient, if unglamorous, pigtails. Wisps of fine, wavy hair had escaped the bands to form a golden halo around her face. She wasn't wearing makeup and her complexion was pale, almost the color of fine porcelain. The pale color of the rest of her face drew attention to her startlingly blue eyes. Had she known she would have a visitor, she most certainly would have colored her cheeks and lips, and changed into something more attractive than the khaki painter's pants and voluminous old shirt she was wearing. She was unaware of the way the shirt hung, revealing the delicate angles of her shoulders and the graceful swell of her bust. The top two buttons were open, revealing the slender base of her neck and a triangle of creamy white chest.

"Let me get my jacket," she said. "I think it's pretty chilly outside."

"You don't have to come out. I'll bring your flashlight back."

"I don't mind. Maybe I can hold the light while you work. Do you have tools?"

"Never leave home without them."

The crisp night air was alive with the chirping of crickets. There hadn't been a hard frost yet and the air was fragrant with fall blossoms and leafy smells. Anne loved every season for its special perfume. Autumn was different from spring and summer. The fall fragrance wasn't as sweet as that of spring, but it had its own slight smoky character. Someone, at a distance, had burned leaves that day. The odor was just a suggestion of smoke mingled with the green foliage smells and the subtle fragrances of fall blooms.

Anne and Jeremy walked side by side as he cast the light on the shoulder of the road ahead of them. His four-wheel-drive Blazer was a few hundred yards down the road from Anne's shop.

"How did you know that I live alone?" Anne asked as they walked.

"I didn't. But the shop has only two rooms. Not much room to raise a family. By the way, do you have a name?"

"Anne Keene, owner and proprietor of Keene's Krafts Kabin."

"Anne . . . a nice name. Since you admit that you do live alone, I can only repeat that you ought to have a phone."

Anne laughed. "Don't start that again."

"How am I going to call you if you don't have a phone?"

"Good question," Anne replied. They reached the truck and Anne held the lantern while Jeremy worked the hood latch. A cloud of steam billowed around them as he raised the hood.

"Point the light down there." He was once again taking charge. His voice resonated with the confidence of one accustomed to giving orders. "Damn, I was afraid of that. The fan belt is completely gone. I was hoping it had only popped off. Well, if I can't get a tow, it's obvious that I'm not going to be moving the car tonight. I'm going to have to take you up on that ride."

"That's all right. It isn't far to the motel."

"Actually, if it wouldn't be too much trouble, I'd rather go the other way."

"What?"

"Up to my house."

"You can't be planning to stay up there tonight," Anne replied incredulously. "The place is all boarded up."

"I know I can't stay there. The power isn't even on. But I came all this way tonight dying to see the place. I haven't been up there in years. It'll take only a couple of minutes to go up there, then you can take me back to the motel."

"What do you expect to see in the dark?"

"We've got a dandy flashlight."

"All right. Let me lock up the shop."

Anne marveled at the way he was taking her over. He had said "we" as if it were a foregone conclusion that this was to be a joint venture into the old house. Anne felt her emotions being pulled in different directions. On the one hand, he was a compelling man. She was going along with his every suggestion only a few minutes after they'd met. It was easy to let him steer their course. He had an air of infallibility.

On the other hand, this was just the kind of domineering man who'd driven her from the city. She had tired of being the assistant, the helpmate, the second banana; she wanted to be responsible for her own life and business. She warned herself that she would have to watch every step with this man. He could easily take over her life and rob her of the independence she wanted so badly.

"Is this all the car you have?" Jeremy broke into her thoughts.

"It may not be a Rolls," Anne said, climbing into the driver's seat of the Bug, "but it will get us where we're going. More than I can say for *your* wheels," she added pointedly.

"It's not getting where we're going that I'm worried about," he replied. "It's getting in. There seems to be more of me than there is of it."

"You'll see, it's magic. It's bigger inside than it is outside." Anne took some pleasure in the cramped position he had to assume to fit his six-foot four-inch frame into the tiny car. Folded up that way, he didn't seem so domineering.

"I didn't know there were any more of these things left on the road."

"You'd be surprised."

"You haven't lived here long, have you?"

"No, I opened my shop last spring. Your name is Breck. I assume you're from around here?"

"Actually, I grew up in Chicago. But my grandfather lived here and I spent all my summers up here."

The trees growing close to the two-lane blacktop highway formed a tunnel of foliage. Anne's headlights forged a path ahead of the car, but the darkness still seemed almost too thick to penetrate. Anne watched the edge of the road carefully, looking for the turnoff to go up to the Breck house. She knew it would be hard to see in the dark. Jeremy noticed her intent searching.

"The drive is easy to find. There's a huge old oak tree right before it. You can't miss it," he offered.

"It was struck by lightning last August," Anne explained. "The highway crew came and took it out. The drive is pretty well grown over, so it may be hard to find."

"The old tree is gone," he mused. "My great-grandfather planted that tree. The woods were all pine back then and he loved hardwoods, so he had that tree brought all the way from Ohio. Grandfather used to say that as long as the tree marked the drive, the Breck family would be an influence in Paradise."

"Your family must have been quite influential."

"More than influential. Great-grandfather owned Paradise and everybody in it. Grandfather tried to hold on to the empire, but the time for that had passed. The Breck fortune was based on the Breck copper mine. Josiah Breck, my great-grandfather, started the mine and branched out into banks, a general store, and logging. Around the turn of the century, the copper played out, but Josiah kept on with the banks and general store. Grandfather was the president of the Miners' Bank of Paradise after Josiah died, but the bank failed in the Great Depression. All that was left was Breck's Mercantile Company. Even that closed its doors in the 1940s, when Grandfather retired. He knew that the time of the Robber Barons was over, so he sent my father away to college rather than take him into the business. I'm afraid that I'm the last living Breck, and all that's left of Josiah Breck's empire and fortune is the old house on the hill."

Anne gave him a sidelong glance. "Do you have a job lined up?"

Jeremy laughed. "I didn't mean that I was impoverished. I've been working and saving my money for years. I've always wanted to come back here and fix up the old house. I'm going to convert it to a country inn."

Anne spotted the drive and made a left turn. The

lane was rough and the bouncing of the little car made conversation impossible for the moment. Anne said a silent prayer that they wouldn't get stuck. The Bug lurched in and out of potholes and swayed back and forth along the deep ruts. Trees and bushes grew close to the drive, which was hardly more than a trail, and scraped along the side of the car. Anne was glad she didn't have a fancy paint job on the car to worry about.

They came out of the woods at the top of the hill and were facing the old house. Anne had come up here one day during the summer just to see the place that everybody talked about. A local legend, the old house was a monument to the will and stubbornness of Josiah Breck. The three-story, Second Empire brick mansion was unique for the area. In a place where pine lumber was abundant, Josiah had insisted on using brick, so the story went. The land in the area was sandy and no decent clay for bricks was available, so Josiah had his bricks brought in by barge from the Lower Peninsula of Michigan. The barges were some of the first cargo carriers to come through the newly completed St. Mary's Canal and through the Soo Locks at Sault Ste. Marie. When Josiah's bricks arrived at the docks in Paradise, the little town was no more than a logging camp. The great house that Josiah erected on the hill was a wonder of the world to the people of the area.

In an age when transportation was expensive and risky, Josiah didn't understand the words "too expensive" or "too far away." He wanted a great brick mansion like the ones he'd seen in Cleveland as a young man, so he built a great brick mansion.

There was no moon, but the stars winked brilliantly in the black void. The house stood out as a dark hulk against the star-sprinkled sky. Anne shivered involuntarily.

"You really want to make this place into an inn? It looks more like a setting for a ghost story than for a honeymoon weekend."

"It's going to be beautiful," Jeremy said calmly. "It will be everything that the Copper Country Resort is not." He referred to a huge vacation complex located about twenty miles west of Paradise. "I stayed there a few years ago when I came up for a visit. That's when I decided to open my own place. What this area needs is a hotel with the ambience and feel of the Upper Peninsula. When you go to any of the big commercial places, you might as well be in downtown Chicago: tennis courts, swimming pools, a four-star gourmet restaurant with overpriced meals you can have anywhere, and nine hundred identical rooms. That's what the Paradise Inn *isn't* going to be.

"It's going to be a place where a honeymooning couple can be by themselves. They can walk in the woods, fish in the lake, see the sights, and in the evening come back to a room that's like a home. There'll be family-style meals and Continental breakfasts. And everybody who comes to the Paradise Inn will know the innkeeper personally. They'll come back year after year to spend their vacations here."

Anne was suddenly uncomfortable. He was being too open with her and, for some reason, he assumed her sympathy. She wished he would be a little more restrained—if only because the extra distance would give her a chance to sort out her feelings.

"That's some pipe dream," she replied vaguely.

"You don't think I can do it?"

"I think the house needs an awful lot of work and I also think the Copper Country Resort will give you stiff competition. Have you ever run a business? It isn't as easy as it may look."

Jeremy raised an eyebrow. "Is that so? My, my." He got out of the car and came around to her side. "Come on," he said. "Let's see how much work the place needs."

"Me? Go in there, in the middle of the night? No, thank you. You go ahead and look around to your heart's content. I'll wait here."

Jeremy opened her car door. "What are you afraid of—ghosts? I suppose you've heard the story that Josiah still strides through the corridors, riding crop tucked under his arm, mouthing commands at long-dead servants."

"No, I hadn't heard that one. But I think I'll pass, all the same."

"I wouldn't think of it." Jeremy reached in and gently pulled Anne from the car. He took her hand firmly in his own as he led her briskly toward the front porch. Anne had to hurry to keep up and avoid being dragged across the overgrown lawn. The dry weeds scratched her ankles as they strode toward the dark porch. Jeremy took the stone steps two at a time and Anne had to run up them to keep pace.

The great, peeling wooden door was blocked by several rough boards nailed haphazardly across the entry. Jeremy pulled on one and the nails parted from the dry wood of the doorjamb easily. He pulled off the other board and, with a large iron key that he withdrew from his pockets, unlocked the door. The key turned with a metallic scrape and a clank. Jeremy was about to push the door open when Anne stopped him.

"Why are you doing this?" she asked.

"I want to see the condition of the place," he answered innocently.

"I mean, why are you dragging me along? You don't need me in there."

"You *are* afraid of ghosts." He laughed.

"I'm no such thing."

"I assure you, any ghosts that live in this house are

friendly ones. I spent the happiest days of my life here." He pushed the door open and it moved with a dry creak. "Hinges need oiling," he said confidently. "I'll strip all this old paint off and refinish it in the natural wood. Wait until you see it—it will be magnificent."

Anne felt an odd shock as he spoke. He was letting her know his renovation plans as if she were going to be around when it was going on. She was beginning to wonder if he was entirely rational—one simply didn't discuss one's whole life with a total stranger. She had half a mind to bolt back to the car and leave him here with his friendly ghosts.

Jeremy cast the beam of the flashlight around the entry hall. A wide staircase with a carved wood banister led to the second floor. A thick layer of dust covered everything, and the floor was strewn with pine cones and little bits of trash and leaves.

"We'll have to find out where the squirrels are getting in," he said, indicating the trash on the floor. "Probably through the chimneys."

"Was this place heated with fireplaces?"

"There are several," he replied, "but the main heat comes from a boiler in the basement. It's original equipment. Central heat was the newest thing when Great-grandfather installed the boiler."

"It will be a miracle if it still works."

"We'll see." He took her hand again and led her through a door into what must have once been the parlor. Most of the furniture was covered with dusty sheets; the sheet on a sofa with gracefully curving wooden legs was askew, revealing a frightfully dusty corner of the upholstery. The shadows of the chairs and tables stretched and wobbled eerily in the beam of light as Jeremy aimed it around the room. Anne was as tense as a coiled spring. She wasn't sure whether it was the house that was making her so or Jeremy's strange behavior. She kept hearing little scratching sounds in the walls and ceiling that she was fairly sure didn't come from squirrels. She took a false step sideways in the dark and bumped against a chair, disturbing something perched on the back of it. Anne was startled by a sudden whirring of wings that brushed her shoulder as something flew toward the ceiling.

She screamed, feeling she would jump out of her skin. Strong arms closed securely around her and drew her near. She buried her face in Jeremy's chest, terrified of what she would see if she looked around. Her heart was pounding and her knees felt weak, but she noticed that Jeremy's chest was solid and that his shirt gave off a wonderfully masculine smell.

"Sh," he said soothingly as he rubbed her back. "It's nothing to be afraid of. Look." He trained the flashlight on the top of a dusty wooden cabinet in the corner. Anne opened her eyes slowly and gingerly moved her head back from Jeremy's chest. A sparrow perched nervously on top of the cabinet. It regarded the couple with a suspicious eye as it danced back and forth from one foot to the other. "See? It's more frightened of us than we are of it."

Anne let out a deep breath and relaxed.

"That bird is a very close friend of mine," he said quietly.

"What?"

"He arranged to have a beautiful woman jump into my arms, didn't he?" Anne stepped back from him, her cheeks burning with a sudden blush.

"I'll wait in the car," she said in her most decisive voice.

"I'll come with you," Jeremy said. "I've seen enough, and I wouldn't want to leave you waiting alone in the dark."

"It's okay. Take your time," Anne said with a breeziness she didn't feel. She turned on her heel and started for the door.

"You don't want to have to feel your way out in the dark, do you?"

Once again, Anne found her hand firmly in his as he led her back out into the night.

Chapter Two

By the time Anne woke up the next morning, the sun was high in the sky. She was usually an early riser, but her adventures of the night before apparently had tired her more than she'd realized. The tattered remnants of a dream of strong arms and gentle caresses fluttered in the recesses of her mind. She sat up and blinked her eyes several times against the bright morning light in her room.

The crafts shop did have only two rooms. The front room was taken up by her salesroom and workshops, and the back one had her bed, a small table, a sink and hot plate, and the old wardrobe she used for a closet. The count of two rooms didn't include the tiny tacked-on bathroom at the back.

Anne had done her best to make the back area into a livable environment. Bright calico curtains hung at the windows and a thick wool rug she'd purchased at a garage sale covered the rough floorboards. The walls were painted a clean, crisp white that set off the bright colors of the stained-glass pieces she had hung around the room. Her bed was covered with a beautiful patchwork crazy quilt, an heirloom passed down from her grandmother.

The room was chilly, as the fire in the stove had long since gone out, and her breath came out in white puffs. Anne slipped from under the covers and ran to the wardrobe for her heavy robe. Once the robe was

pulled tightly around her and her slippers were on
her feet, Anne went to the wood bin to get a log for
the fire. She took some kindling and a medium-sized
log, and carefully arranged them in the stove on top of
some crumpled newspaper. She lit the corner of the
paper and stood waiting for the fire to get going while
she blew on her hands and danced from foot to foot to
keep warm. It had never been this cold in the morning before.

Anne glanced at a window and saw that a frost had
come late the night before; the edges of the glass
panes were decorated with a frost forest. The sun
shone through the window bringing the crystals to
brilliant life. She went over and blew a puff of warm
air onto the glass, watching the bright crystals grow
into the circle of moisture. Rubbing a small patch
clear on the window, she peeked out into a world
festooned with jewels of frozen dew.

The leaves were just beginning to turn to their
autumn hues of orange, yellow, and red. The remaining green summer leaves, the brilliant autumn leaves,
and the dry weeds near the ground were all outlined
in sparkling crystals. Anne marveled at the beauty
that surrounded her little shop. Her stained-glass creations paled in comparison.

As soon as the fire had driven back the chill, she
dressed and made a light breakfast of tea and toast.
She spent some time tidying up her living quarters,
then went out to polish some of the glass pieces in the
shop. The pieces needed periodic attention to keep
them bright and attractive for customers, customers
that will never come, Anne thought bitterly. Next
spring, when the tourists came back, she wouldn't be
here.

She was determined to stand her ground until the
last of her cash ran out. She owed her dream that
much. But then what? The idea of going back to her

old employer, Mr. Masters, and begging for her old job back stuck in her throat. Old Mr. Masters was kind enough, and her accountant's position in his CPA firm paid well, but she had all but suffocated under his kindly, fatherly attentions. Mr. Masters, a successful businessman in his late fifties, had controlled every aspect of her work. She was one of eight young accountants working for him and he treated them all the same way. When you worked for Mr. Masters, you might write down the answers, but he told you exactly what to do to arrive at them, every step of the way. He never left anything to another's discretion.

Anne's discontent had been fed by the fact that she didn't particularly like her work. A college counselor had urged her into accounting because it offered a good prospect of steady employment and because she was good at math. Once Anne started working at the job, however, she found it dull. Not unbearably dull, for Anne was a steady worker with a high tolerance for detail, but totally lacking in excitement.

The excitement in her life came from her hobby—stained glass. She had taken an adult education course in the subject at the community center and was instantly fascinated with the bright, jewellike pieces of glass and the way they could be built together with lead "came" to make a work of art. From that moment on, every spare moment was spent designing and making her stained-glass creations.

Before long, Anne's friends had all the stained glass they had space for. She managed to take some orders for pieces through classified ads she placed in newspapers, but the business wasn't enough to support her. As long as she had to work full time for Mr. Masters, she wouldn't have time to make her artwork her career.

Moving to Paradise, Michigan, had been a dream she'd nurtured since childhood. Her family had spent all their vacations here when she was young. To Anne no sky was bluer than the sky over Paradise, no air smelled sweeter, no hiking trails were a lusher green, and no fish tasted better than those her father used to catch from his little aluminum rowboat.

Every summer her family spent two weeks in a rented cottage just a few miles from the lake. Year after year, her father would swear that he was going to save his money to buy their own cottage, where he could retire, but someday never came. Anne had held on to the dream, and when she started to plan for the day when she would quit her dull accounting job and go into business for herself, she knew that only one place would do for her stained-glass shop—Paradise.

Anne chuckled as she remembered a television weatherman's joke: "it's colder than Hell in Paradise in the morning." Michigan boasted not only a town called Paradise, but in the Lower Peninsula there was also a town called Hell. A waggish weatherman would always say, "It's colder than Hell in Paradise," whenever the appropriate temperatures prevailed in the two cities.

About mid-morning, Anne heard a motor outside and peeked out to see Mort's wrecker hook up Jeremy's Blazer and tow it away. As the vehicles disappeared from sight Anne thought that, with all the physical evidence gone, the adventure of the night before might have been a dream. But Jeremy Breck was much too real to be dismissed from her mind so easily. She found herself thinking of him over and over again.

His dream was so much like her own. She knew now that that was what had bothered her so much about Jeremy's personal revelations last night. She had to be very careful not to get caught up in his plans. Her own failed dream was about all the failure Anne wanted to have to live with; she didn't want to have to bear the weight of his failure as well.

Anne had a feeling that he would soon be finding

out the truths that had come so painfully to her over the past summer. He would find out that customers don't show up just because you've opened a business; business loans were hard to come by; and the U-pers, the proud natives of the Upper Peninsula, didn't open their hearts and homes to outsiders. "Outsider" meant anyone not born in the area.

Jeremy was full of enthusiasm and confidence, but Anne knew that confidence wasn't enough. She would have to shield herself from the disappointment that he was sure to experience.

After lunching on a peanut butter and jelly sandwich, Anne was about to go into town and see if she had any mail at the post office when there was a knock on her door. Her heart told her it was Jeremy, and the quickening of her pulse disturbed her.

She opened the door and found, to her surprise, a man she didn't know. He was dressed in workman's overalls, and various tools hung in his belt.

"Can I help you?" she asked, masking an irrational disappointment.

"I'm here to install your phone," the man answered brusquely.

"I didn't order a phone," Anne replied, puzzled.

"I have a signed work order right here," he said, pulling a folded sheet of paper from his pocket. "The order only came in this morning—one here and one up at the old Breck place. There aren't many buildings out here. I'm sure this is the one."

Anne was sure that she knew who had ordered the phone. She was amused at the joke but annoyed at the inconvenience of having to send the man away.

"Look, I think I know what's going on," Anne said pleasantly. "It's just a little joke. I don't want a phone."

"Look, lady. It's cold out here. Couldn't I come inside? I have a signed order here. I don't make them out, I just install phones. When I get a work order, I install a phone. See how it works?"

Anne allowed the man to step inside to continue the argument. "I understand that you're not responsible, but you have to understand that I didn't order a phone. You wouldn't want to install a phone for someone who can't afford it, would you? You'd just have to come back in a few days and take it back out again."

"The installation, deposit, and first month's bill are all prepaid. See?" He pointed to a section of the work order.

"But I still couldn't afford to pay the monthly bill," Anne exclaimed in exasperation. There didn't seem to be any way to get through to the man.

"Look, lady. I don't want to know your problems. They're none of my business. I just install phones. Your personal arrangements are entirely up to you. All I know is that bills for both phones are supposed to go to the Breck house."

Anne didn't know what to say. She couldn't believe that anybody would do such a crazy thing.

"Where do you want it?"

"I don't know," Anne replied dumbly.

"How about behind the counter?" he suggested. "A lot of businesses have the phone behind the counter."

Anne nodded and sat down at her worktable while the phoneman went to work. About an hour later, after he had climbed the pole outside the shop and connected her line, the installation was complete. The workman handed her a copy of the work order and left.

As the man shut the door behind himself Anne stood staring at the intrusive object in her shop. Almost as if it had been planned, the phone rang.

"Hello?"

"Anne, I see you got the phone." The rich tone of Jeremy's voice came through even over the wires.

"How *dare* you," Anne sputtered. "How do you know that the reason I don't have a phone isn't because I don't like to be bothered by obnoxious callers?"

"But you have a phone now. As I said last night, if you don't have one, how can I call you?"

"You assume an awful lot," Anne snapped.

"Now, now, calm down. I do have a legitimate reason for calling."

"Well?" Anne replied impatiently.

"I'd like you to come up to the house."

"No, thank you. I saw enough of the house last night."

"I have a business proposal to present to you. And when you come," he continued confidently, "bring that stained-glass parrot you have hanging near the door of your shop. I want to buy it."

"That piece costs one hundred and fifty dollars," Anne said coldly.

"I'll have a check ready for you," he said casually. "Be here at three, okay?" And before she could answer, Jeremy hung up.

Anne had to pause and think. She couldn't let Jeremy take over her life, but the sale of the parrot would mean at least an extra two weeks that she could stay in Paradise. She had no idea what kind of business proposal he could have in mind, but she decided firmly that if the proposal was a job in his inn, she would turn him down flat.

Anne realized that the only safe approach to Mr. Jeremy Breck would be to appear so businesslike that he couldn't possibly turn the meeting into anything personal. She went to her wardrobe and chose one of her "authority" outfits that she wore when she worked for Mr. Masters. It had never worked then, she had to admit, but then, nothing worked on Mr. Masters.

She put on a gray wool flannel suit with a straight skirt and a tailored jacket. The jacket had a mandarin collar that fit nicely around the base of her neck and a small breast pocket, into which she placed a burgundy silk handkerchief. She put on burgundy low-heeled pumps and picked up a matching clutch purse. Brushing the pigtails out of her fine, blond hair, Anne pulled it back from her face with a pair of tortoise-shell combs.

She applied her most businesslike makeup: a hint of blusher on the cheekbones, fawn-brown mascara to accentuate her pale lashes, and wine-colored lipstick. When she finished, she examined herself in the mirror, satisfied that she looked professional and businesslike.

Anne wrapped the parrot carefully in tissue paper and placed it in a box that she tied with string. At ten of three, she put on her coat, got in her car, and drove up to the Breck house. She picked her way across the overgrown lawn carefully, wanting to avoid runs in her stockings. With the parrot box tucked under her arm, she rapped firmly on the mansion door.

"Excellent. You're punctual," Jeremy exclaimed as he opened the door. It opened smoothly, without a sound. Obviously he had already oiled the hinges.

Jeremy took her coat and hung it on a coat tree in the corner of the entry hall. As he turned back to face her he stopped and inspected her thoroughly, up and down. Before he could speak and say something embarrassingly complimentary about her looks, Anne spoke.

"The parrot, Mr. Breck," she said as she handed him the box.

"Fine. Here's your check." He pulled his checkbook out of the back pocket of his jeans and wrote one out. Anne noticed that he was filthy from head to toe. There were festoons of cobwebs and dust in his hair and mustache, and gray smears all over his face. His clothes were dusty and wrinkled.

"By the way, call me Jeremy. I thought we were well past the 'Mr.' stage."

Anne examined the check. "Wait a minute. This is drawn on a bank in Chicago," she said.

"Of course. I arrived only last night and haven't had time to move my account yet. I assure you it won't bounce."

"The bank in town will want to hold it until it clears," Anne replied.

"If you're hard up for immediate cash, I have some traveler's checks."

"No, that won't be necessary," Anne said quickly, not wanting to let him know just how desperate her financial condition was. She didn't need the money immediately.

"You said you had a business proposition," Anne said.

"All in good time," Jeremy replied with a smile. "You put me to shame. If you'll hold on for a couple of minutes, I'll clean up a little."

"I came up here on business," Anne replied coolly. "You don't need to change."

"Business." He chuckled. "Do I need an appointment to tell you that you look absolutely beautiful today?"

Anne blushed. "Would you care to state your business?" she said, trying to sound unflustered.

"All in good time," he repeated. "Come down to the kitchen. I've got it partially cleaned up and there's a chair you can sit on without spoiling your skirt. Have a cup of coffee, and before you know it, I'll be ready to talk business."

Anne followed him helplessly down the hall. "I see you've made quite a bit of progress, for just one day," she said as they walked.

"I've got the utilities turned on, some of the boards

off the windows, and I've cleaned up a few spots. I intend to stay here tonight."

The kitchen was swept, dusted, and wiped down. It needed paint and probably some new fixtures. The sink was badly rusted and the windows were cloudy with years of grime. The linoleum floor was cracked and curling around the edges, but it was scrupulously clean.

Anne chuckled. "You did a beautiful job on this floor. Do you do windows?"

Jeremy winked back at her and stepped into a bathroom off the kitchen. She heard water running as he started to wash up.

"Coffee's on the stove," he called out to her from the bathroom. "I'm sorry to make you wait, but I wanted to get as much work done as possible before you got here. There's so much to do."

Anne found a clean cup in the drainer next to the sink and poured a cup of coffee from the carafe on the stove. A few minutes later, Jeremy stepped out of the bathroom, in the process of pulling a clean knit shirt over his head.

"By the way, you were right," he said cheerfully. "The boiler is shot. I'll have to buy a new one."

While the shirt was still above his broad shoulders Anne got a glimpse of a muscular chest sporting a thick covering of curly black hair. He pulled the shirt down smoothly and adjusted the collar.

"Speaking of putting things in," Anne said evenly. "That phone in my shop is going to have to go."

"Why?"

"I can't afford it."

"It isn't costing you anything."

"I can't let you pay my phone bill. What are you going to do if I start running up huge bills calling people in Rumania and Fort Wayne, Indiana?"

"Do you know anybody in Rumania or Fort Wayne?"

"That's not the point, but you know what I mean. We hardly know each other. All I did last night was offer you a ride. You can't start paying my bills."

"I'll make you a deal," he replied playfully. "Forget Rumania and you can call Fort Wayne anytime you want."

"*Jeremy,*" Anne exclaimed in frustration. "Why on earth do you want to pay for a phone in my shop?"

"I told you. You shouldn't be living there alone without a phone. Besides, I put it in for my own convenience. I wanted to call you."

"I suppose that if you ever wanted to call an Eskimo at the North Pole, you'd have lines strung up there," Anne replied.

"Only if you were that Eskimo."

"The phone has to go," Anne said stubbornly.

"Look, leave it in for one month," he said reasonably. "Then, if you still don't want it, have it taken out. Since I've already paid the installation fee and the first month's bill, it would be a waste to pull it out right away."

Anne wondered what it took to break through his shell of confidence.

"Now," he said, "let's get down to business. Have you ever done any really big stained-glass windows?"

"I did a bay window for my old boss in Detroit."

"Good, then you should be able to handle what I need."

He led her from the kitchen to a large room at the back of the house. Jeremy had pulled the boards off the windows and several were without glass. A chilly wind blew through the room.

The room had once been a beautiful, well-stocked library. There was a huge marble-manteled fireplace at one end of the room, and the walls were lined with dusty bookshelves. The books were in deplorable condition, moldy, decaying, and dirty. Jeremy hadn't gotten around to cleaning this room yet, and the furniture was still covered with sheets.

"Won't you be cold sleeping here tonight?" Anne asked, shivering.

"My room upstairs still has the glass in the windows, and I'll keep a fire going tonight. Which reminds me—could you lend me some wood? I noticed that you have a good-sized woodpile by your shop. I could return the wood in a few days, after I'm more settled."

"I don't suppose I could begrudge you wood for your bedroom fireplace," Anne replied. "Do you need me to bring it up?"

"No, I'll come down and get it. My truck is fixed."

"Which window do you want done?"

"These three," Jeremy said, indicating the west wall of the library. Anne's eyes opened wide when she saw what he wanted. He was pointing to a huge empty frame, eight feet high by nine feet wide, flanked by two small narrow frames.

Anne took a deep breath. "I've never done anything that big before," she said.

"Can you do it?"

"It depends on the design you want. There will have to be several solid supports to break it up and give it enough strength." She thought for a moment. "I suppose I could do it in three vertical panels for the main window."

"How long will it take?"

"Quite a while. I'll have to order the glass because I don't have enough in stock for anything this size. Once I've got the materials, a month or so. But this is going to be expensive. The materials alone will run me several hundred dollars. I'd have to take a sharp pencil to it, and it will depend a lot on the design you want, but I don't think I could do it for less than two thousand for the center window and one thousand for each of the side windows."

"Fine. How much do you need in advance?"

"Well, first let's see what sort of design you want. The more detailed a design is, the more solder and time are required, and some colors of glass are more expensive than others."

"For the center panel I want a reproduction of the original window. I guess the original windows were broken or stolen during the years when the house stood vacant. I have a photograph of the old window. It was the most magnificent thing north of Toledo back when Josiah had it put in. It was made in Europe and he had it specially designed. They brought it by mule boat down the Erie Canal, then shipped it by the Great Lakes to Paradise."

"How do you know all this?"

"Josiah kept journals and I've read them all. He always wrote down the details of how he did things." Jeremy picked up an old photo album from a sheet-covered table. He must have brought the album with him, Anne assumed, because it was clean and in good condition.

"You can see most of the center window in this picture. Unfortunately I don't have any pictures of the side panels. I'll lave them to your discretion. As I remember, they were floral designs."

The photograph showed a small boy standing on the sill in front of the big window. He appeared to be four or five years old and was spreading his arms and grinning at the camera.

"Is this you?"

"Never mind the kid. Can you do the design?"

"It is you, isn't it? You were cute."

Jeremy moved up behind her to look over her shoulder at the album. She could feel the warmth of his body close to hers, and his breath ruffled the hair at her ears.

"Some people say I still am," he replied.

"I wouldn't touch that line with a ten-foot pole." Anne laughed. She couldn't prevent herself from enjoying his company, but she reminded herself sternly of her resolve to keep the meeting on business. She looked at the window in the photo; it was a picture of a sunset over the hill where the Breck house stood.

"This is black and white. I can't tell what colors I'll need."

"I remember the colors and I'll describe them to you." His voice was terribly close to her ear and he had practically whispered his reply.

"It's a very complicated design. I'm afraid it will run more than two thousand."

"Price is no object. I'm sure you can do it cheaper than if I had it made in Europe and shipped by mule boat."

"You'll need to cover the window frames in the meantime. This room is in bad enough condition without the wind and snow coming in."

"I'll take care of it," Jeremy replied. His attention seemed far from the problem of the windows. Anne turned to face him in an attempt to recapture his attention, but she could see right away that she'd never lost it. It was what she was saying that he wasn't paying attention to.

"I won't be able to order the glass until your check clears."

"I'll phone my bank in Chicago and have a direct transfer made," Jeremy replied in a totally bemused voice.

"Well, then," Anne said, clearing her throat and taking a few steps away from Jeremy. She felt like ducking under one of the dusty sheets to avoid his unnerving stare. Her cheeks flushed to a color much deeper than the subtle blusher she had applied as his gaze settled around her like a cocoon that tightened and seemed to prevent her from catching her breath.

"You'll have to tell me something about the colors so I can make my order," she said as she looked back at the picture. Jeremy came close beside her and took one side of the photo album.

"The sky is blue, much like the color of your eyes," he said in an almost hypnotic voice. Anne was suddenly self-conscious about her eyes and had to resist the impulse to blink. "The bottoms of the clouds are rosy pink, not quite as pink as your cheeks are right now. The pine forest is in several shades of deep green."

"Aha, I've got you there. I haven't got anything green," Anne said, trying to sound breezy but revealing more of her discomfort than she cared to.

"Two out of three isn't bad," Jeremy replied with a smile. He took the album from her hands and set it aside.

Without speaking, he turned and took her face in his large, smooth hands. His fingers felt smooth against Anne's cheeks. As his face descended toward hers she recognized the discomfort she had been feeling as longing. She longed for the touch of his lips. As if he'd read her mind, Jeremy lowered his head. His mustache tickled as it brushed her upper lip, then his warm, moist mouth closed on hers and she lost all contact with her surroundings. She was no longer aware of the chilly breeze coming through the open window frames, and the dusty furniture and decaying books were gone. All she was aware of was the warm, solid body next to hers and the wonderful tingling sensation of his hand as it slid away from her cheek to trace a delicate line over her ear, down the side of her neck, to circle her shoulders and draw her into a tight embrace. His tongue flicked teasingly at her lips, then probed inside to find the sensitive lining of her mouth. Anne's teeth parted invitingly, begging for him to probe more deeply. Her heart pounded in her chest and she felt that she must be glowing with the warmth that radiated through her body.

One of Jeremy's hands found the brass buttons of Anne's suit jacket and began slowly, seductively, to unfasten them, staring at her neck and working his way down. A cold breeze now penetrated her thin blouse, and Anne suddenly remembered where she was and what she was doing.

"Stop," she cried, pushing him away with a quick burst of strength.

"You're right," he replied huskily. "It's too cold in here. It's warmer upstairs." He took her hand and began to lead her from the room. Anne planted her feet firmly and refused to be led. She hurriedly rebuttoned her jacket and smoothed her hair. Her blush had abruptly turned to acute embarrassment.

"What's the matter?" Jeremy asked, sounding almost annoyed at her sudden change of attitude.

"I'll thank you to keep your hands to yourself," Anne fumed. She felt slightly guilty as she spoke, for she knew she'd made no attempt to resist his advances. "I'll have you know that I don't fall for every man who orders a window. I don't even *know* you. I think I'd better be going now."

"I think you know that this isn't a casual conquest, Anne," Jeremy said seriously. "We're going to work together and make this enterprise work. We're going to be partners."

"Oh, no, you're not sucking me into this. We're relative strangers. You came to my door last night to use the phone, remember? Your pie-in-the-sky dreams of a country inn are all yours—I want no part of them."

"Does that mean you won't do the window?"

"I'll do the window. I'll do it because I need the money, and that's the only reason. When you come down tonight to pick up the firewood, I'll show you my glass samples and you can pick the colors. And if you try to touch anything but the glass, I'll use the phone you so thoughtfully installed to call the police."

"Very well," Jeremy replied in a calm, even voice. He reached into his back pocket and drew out his checkbook, wrote one out, and handed it to Anne.

"What?" she said as she looked at the check for $7,000. "I need only a thousand to get started. This is more than I quoted you for the whole job."

"You just said you needed the money," Jeremy said evenly. "There will be a bonus if you can finish the window before Christmas."

Anne stared at Jeremy incredulously. He *must* be out of his mind, she thought.

"You aren't going to last long if this is how you do business," Anne said after a pause.

"It's not so bad as it seems," he said, with an infuriatingly charming smile. "I'd have to pay more than ten thousand if I were to get a contractor anywhere else to do it, and I consider the restoration of this window to be one of the most important aspects of this renovation. Besides, I intend to get my money's worth."

Chapter Three

Anne let the $7,000 check sit on her desk for a full day before she made up her mind to deposit it in her account. Signing the back and handing it to a bank teller seemed to constitute an acceptance of Jeremy's intention to get his "money's worth." Anne had a strong feeling that he wasn't talking about glass, and that was the dilemma.

On one hand, the check was the means to turn her failing business and dream into a success. After buying her materials, she'd have plenty left to carry her well into the next tourist season. But she also felt as if accepting the money constituted giving up her independence. She would be able to stay in Paradise in her shop, not because of her ability or her business sense but because Jeremy had decided to sponsor her. That was what the check constituted—sponsorship. He was paying her more than the job was worth so she'd have enough money to stay.

Anne reviewed every moment of their acquaintance, looking for some reason why Jeremy had latched onto her. He was a devastatingly attractive man, and under less forced circumstances Anne might have welcomed his advances, but there seemed no logical reason why he would simply walk into her shop one night and take over her life. She saw herself as an attractive woman, not devastating like Jeremy, but certainly attractive. But somehow she knew it wasn't just her looks that made him act as he did.

Jeremy was a mystery and Anne was fascinated by the contradictions he seemed to present. He was also dangerous to her. That was the lesson she'd learned in the library. His touch excited her in a way she had never dreamed possible, and she knew she'd have to watch herself every moment she was with him. Doing the windows, she would be with him a lot, going to the house many times in order to complete the job. Dealing with Jeremy Breck was going to require every bit of self-control and discipline she could muster.

And so Anne debated with herself until she finally gave up and deposited the check, then ordered the glass. Three days later, she found herself being summoned back to the house. Jeremy called to inform her that the carpenter was there and she would be needed to supervise the installation of the window frames. Anne dressed in jeans and a heavy flannel shirt, and went to the house ready to work in the dusty, dirty library.

As she pulled up the hill she saw that the house had undergone a transformation. The weeds and burrs that had choked the overgrown lawn were gone and the ground had been tilled for a new lawn. A flagstone walk, previously invisible under the weeds, marked the way to the porch.

After a brief cold snap the weather had turned warm and sunny again. A crew of painters were taking advantage of the Indian summer to paint the wooden gingerbread around the windows and porch of the old brick house. Vans belonging to half a dozen contractors were parked along the drive, and the house buzzed with activity.

As she walked in the open front door Anne had to dodge the carpet layers who were replacing the faded, dirty carpet in the entry hall and on the stairs. The air was full of hollow pounding, and Anne wondered briefly why anyone would be hammering on the pipes. Jeremy met her in the hall, gesturing around at the work in progress. He was dressed in an old chambray shirt and a pair of jeans.

"It's coming right along," he shouted over the din.

"What's all that pounding?" Anne shouted back.

"The new furnace. The sound of the men working carries right through the pipes."

"What?" Anne shouted.

Jeremy took her elbow and led her down the hall. The library turned out to be as full of activity as the entry had been. Several workmen were busy loading up and removing the old furniture.

"Are you replacing all this furniture?" Anne asked in a slightly lower voice. If nothing else, the library was a little quieter.

"No, I'm just having it reupholstered and refinished. Most of these pieces are antiques and too valuable to get rid of."

Anne could see that Jeremy had been hard at work in this room since she had last stood here. The floor had been swept, the shelves dusted, and the books were stacked in the center of the room, where he'd been sorting through them to find any that were in good enough condition to be valuable.

"It's a shame that so many of those books were ruined," Anne said.

"Well, I've found a few that are worth saving. I'll have to work on refilling the shelves with a new collection of my own."

The carpenter and his helper waited by the open window frames.

"I'm tellin' you, Mr. Breck. What you want in here are triple-glazed louvered windows. They'll keep your heat bill down in the winter and you can open them up for a nice breeze in the summer. You ain't used to living up here in the north country. Everything's got to be insulated. You put this fancy-pants window you're talking about in and you're going to get et alive by the heat bills. Now, my brother-in-law can fix you up with a real good price on triple-glazed windows."

"I'm sure he could," Jeremy said dryly.

"This ain't like Chicago," the man urged.

"It sure ain't." Jeremy chuckled. "But this house was up here long before your brother-in-law went into the glass business and it always had stained glass in here."

"Whatever you say," the carpenter said. "But you're gonna be sorry."

Anne took several minutes to explain exactly what she needed in the way of window frames. To match the originals, they had to be hand built and of wood. The spaces would be filled with plain glass for the time being, and Anne would replace each clear-glass pane with a stained-glass panel as she finished it. The carpenter indicated that he understood what she needed and went to work, slightly morose over having lost the sale of insulated, triple-glazed windows. When Anne finished with the carpenter, she found Jeremy leaning against the fireplace watching her intently. He seemed to approve of the way she dealt with the workman. His smile was pleasant, without any hint of derision.

"Why is it that you can get all this done, but I never see you work?" Anne asked humorously. She felt safe making friendly conversation now because Jeremy could hardly make a pass with the house full of workmen.

"When you're around, I can't seem to get anything done," he replied with his tempting smile. He seemed to be inviting her to ignore the workmen and fall into his waiting arms. "Come here, I want to show you something."

He led her out of the library and back down the hall to the room they'd entered that first night. The room was bare of furniture and had been thoroughly cleaned. A new Oriental rug was spread on the clean hardwood floor. The windows had been washed but still lacked curtains. The only ornament in the room was the stained-glass parrot Jeremy had purchased from her four days earlier. He had mounted it, hanging it from the ceiling near the center of the room. It sparkled like a cut jewel in the light from the window.

"What are you going to do with this room?" Anne asked, trying to sound politely interested.

"It's going to be the main dining room. Aren't you going to ask about the bird?"

Anne wanted to laugh and cry at the same time. It was impossible to maintain a professional distance from Jeremy. He drew her into friendly conversation like a magnet.

"All right, what about the bird?" Anne chuckled.

"Can't you see? I mounted it right over the spot where the sparrow startled you the other night. It shall forever more mark the spot where I first held you in my arms."

"Jeremy," Anne said in humorous exasperation. "I'm here on business."

"Oh," he said with mock disappointment. "Then you're going to miss out on the absolutely marvelous afternoon I have planned for us."

"I think I ought to get back to my shop and go to work."

"You haven't got the glass yet. How can you get to work?"

"I can start laying out my patterns and cutting my templates."

"You can do that tomorrow. The glass won't arrive for a week at least. You can't be contemplating shutting yourself into your shop on what may be the last truly gorgeous afternoon of the year."

"The weatherman says this Indian summer is going to last at least four more days."

"But what if he's wrong? It would be a crime against nature to waste a day like this."

Anne forced the smile away from her lips and replied in her most businesslike tone, "I meant what I said. I'm here on business." She turned to go, but Jeremy blocked her way. His face was every bit as serious as she had been trying to look, and she found him just a little intimidating.

"Anne, I realize I made a serious mistake by coming on too strong with you the other day, and I wish you'd give me a chance to make it up to you. Give me a chance to prove that I'm really a very nice person. All I have in mind is a leisurely picnic. I have some wine and cheese and bread all packed up. We can go over to Tahquamenon Falls, and I give you my word that I won't make any passes you're not receptive to. I think it would be a great chance to overcome your main objection—that we don't know each other. Now, don't tell me that you're going to walk out of here and turn down a wonderful afternoon in the company of a charming man."

Jeremy's serious look melted into one of his irresistibly charming smiles. "Come on, Anne. Admit it. You kind of like me," he said teasingly.

Anne couldn't help but laugh. "How could I help liking you? You're like a huge puppy dog. Only I know that you're a wolf in puppy dog's clothing."

"Oh, but I'm an awfully nice wolf."

Later, in Jeremy's Blazer, driving to the falls, Anne wondered how she had allowed herself to be talked into going.

"So," Jeremy said, "I've won you over."

"Don't get cocky." Anne chuckled. "I've just decided to live dangerously. Or maybe I think I owe you a date because of the check you gave me the other day."

"If that check was purchasing female companionship, you're the most expensive date I've ever had."

"Was it?"

Jeremy avoided the question. "On the other hand, if I was buying a window, I still think I got a bargain."

"You're impossible. Why me? Do you date all your contractors?"

"Hardly. Actually, you're the only woman I know in Paradise at the moment. Is that a good enough reason?"

"I'll accept that tentatively, for the moment."

Even the guard shack at the entrance to the park was deserted. A sign in the window directed visitors to go to the ranger station if they needed assistance. Jeremy drove in and followed the road signs to a parking lot near the lower falls. The picnic lunch was in a knapsack that Jeremy nimbly slipped over his shoulders as they got out of the Blazer.

"The best view of the lower falls is from the island," Jeremy explained. "We'll rent a boat and row across the river."

"I know. I've been here before."

"I'll bet you have," Jeremy said with a smile. "Tell me, what made you decide to open a crafts shop just two miles from my house?"

Jeremy draped an arm around Anne's shoulders in a friendly, gently possessive manner.

"Probably for the same reason you came here," she answered seriously as they walked to the footpath. "I used to come up here with my family when I was little and I always wanted to come back to stay."

"Ah, see? You claim we don't know each other, yet we practically grew up together."

Anne laughed. "Neat trick—growing up together without ever meeting."

The footpath wound its way between blazing orange, yellow, and red autumn trees to the boat-rental concession. The path was deep in dry leaves that

rattled under their feet like Christmas tissue paper.
The boat attendant sat reading a book next to the
dock, where about a dozen rowboats were tied. It
didn't look as if any of the boats were missing.

"We'd like a boat," Jeremy said as they approached
the man.

"Two dollars," the attendant replied.

"It doesn't look like you've got much business today,"
Jeremy said pleasantly as he handed the man the
money.

"Don't get much except on weekends after Labor
Day. I'll only be out here another week or so."

"It's a shame that more people don't take advantage
of this in the fall," Anne said. "I think it's the most
beautiful time of the year."

"It's not a shame at all," Jeremy replied. "We can
have the river all to ourselves."

"About the only ones who make it out here during
the week at this time of year are young lovers and
retired folk," the boatman said. Anne knew which
category the attendant was putting them in.

Jeremy took Anne's hand to steady her as she stepped
into the boat. He took the center bench and put the
oars in the water. Anne sat in the back of the boat
facing him. The water was like liquid amber and the
sun glinted off tiny ripples, making the surface sparkle as it swirled around the oars and sides of the boat.
It was only a short distance to the island, but Jeremy
swung the boat off the straight course and started
rowing upstream, past the island. He rowed with
strong, smooth strokes, forcing the boat to shoot forward with each pull. Anne put her hand over the side
of the boat, dragging her fingers through the golden
water, enjoying the cold wetness and the bright fall
colors that surrounded her.

"I wonder what makes the water this golden color,"
she said idly.

"The color leaches out of fallen trees in the riverbed," Jeremy answered confidently. "That also causes the foam at the foot of the falls." Jeremy took a few more powerful strokes at the oars, then lifted them from the water to let the boat drift gracefully back to the island.

"So, what do you want to know?" Jeremy said with a lazy, relaxed smile.

"About what?"

"About me. You complained that you hardly know me."

"Well, if it's question-and-answer time, I'd love to know what it was that you did for a living that allowed you to save up enough money to do the kind of complete remodeling you're doing at the house."

Jeremy chuckled. "You really do have a practical mind. I bet you've had your little mental calculator going, figuring up exactly how much I'm spending." He didn't sound annoyed or insulted; he was just stating a fact. "Okay, how much do you figure I'm spending?"

"Well, with the window, the carpets, the lawn work, the painters, the furnace, and the reupholstering, I'd say I saw at least fifty thousand dollars' worth today alone."

"Very good. I can see you've got a head for figures and an accurate sense of what things cost. Those are important qualities in a businesswoman." The boat swirled in a lazy circle, ending up drifting backward. "Actually, by the time I'm through, with the plastering and painting, the new wallpaper for downstairs and the bedrooms, the new wiring and plumbing, and the kitchen renovations, I figure the whole job is going to come to about one hundred thousand."

"So, I ask again, did you actually save up all that money, and what did you do for a living?"

"Very direct. You can't be diverted from the question at hand, can you?" He chuckled. "Well, actually,

the other night when I was talking about working and
saving my money, I was speaking figuratively. I'm
paying for most of this work with a bank loan. And in
answer to your second question, I worked for a bank."

"I'm amazed. The Breck name must still carry some
weight in Paradise. I tried to get a measly ten-thousand-
dollar business loan and was turned down flat."

"At the Bank of Paradise?"

"Of course."

"That was your mistake. They don't know you here.
You should have applied for your loan at the bank
where you did your business before you came up here,
where they knew you."

"Still, a hundred-thousand-dollar loan is a pretty
big risk."

"I was considered a very good credit risk at my
bank in Chicago. You see, I was the president before I
quit to come up here. A lot of my salary, back then,
came in the form of stock options and such. I put up
my portfolio as collateral."

"I see," Anne replied. "And if the Paradise Inn
doesn't work out and you can't make the payments?"

Jeremy laughed. It was as if the idea were patently
ridiculous. "Then I'll be penniless and we'll have to
go back to Chicago and you'll have to go to work as a
waitress in a greasy-spoon restaurant to support us
while I drink myself into oblivion in shame and
unemployment."

Anne laughed. "Wait a minute. You're several steps
ahead of me. First, if you head back to Chicago in
defeat, I seriously doubt that I'll go with you. Second,
if I do have to go to work to support us, it will be as an
accountant. That's my profession."

"Funny, I thought you were an artist."

"Currently. But if this doesn't work out, I suppose
I'll be back to crunching numbers."

"That's your trouble, Anne. You came up here to

start a new life and brought your old life with you. Your new life can't take off and fly until you unload the extra baggage and look to the future instead of the past."

"Flying is fine, but it's nice to have a safety net," Anne said seriously.

"I disagree. Once you know what you want, you have to go for it. Hanging back to be safe only keeps what you want out of your grasp."

Uncomfortable, Anne changed the subject. "You seem quite young to be the president of a Chicago bank. I suppose you're a financial genius?"

"I'm thirty-eight. Being a Harvard MBA helped, but marrying the daughter of the chairman of the board clinched the deal."

"You're married?" Anne asked with a raised eyebrow.

"Divorced. I divorced Jean and the bank at the same time."

"Ah, I see you're not above marrying in order to get the job you want."

"Not exactly. Actually, I think it was the other way around. I was a district loan officer when I caught the eye of the chairman. He decided that I'd be a good prospect to take over the bank when he retired. The old man wanted to keep control of the bank in the family, so I was introduced to Jean, then groomed to become her husband and president of the bank."

"But Jean turned out to be a witch and you finally ran away from her and the bank."

"No, not exactly," Jeremy said slowly. "Jean wasn't a witch, but I didn't love her, and I didn't love the bank. As the old man's retirement got closer and closer it became obvious to me, and to Jean, that she and the bank deserved someone who was truly dedicated to the continuation of the family business. We parted on amicable terms. I think they're going to solve the problem by having Jean take over as chairman of the board. She'll put her heart into it, and that's what the bank needs."

Jeremy put the oars back in the water and guided the boat to a landing on the island. He stepped out first and pulled the boat firmly up onto the shore, then offered a hand to Anne as she stepped from the boat. The island was thickly forested with hiking trails cutting between the trees. The forest floor was deeply carpeted with yellow and red leaves and others floated lazily through the air toward the ground. Yellow shafts of light cut through the still air and the scent of leaves and wood and water created a heady perfume. Anne and Jeremy walked silently along a path to a cascade of amber water. A flat rock overlooked the falls and Jeremy slipped the knapsack off and laid the picnic food out on the smooth stone platform.

He spread a red-checkered tablecloth on the ground, then drew two carefully packed crystal wineglasses from the pack. A bottle of Burgundy wine followed the glasses, then a loaf of crusty French bread, a slab of yellow cheese, and some apples. Jeremy uncorked the wine and filled the glasses. The afternoon sun caught the crimson liquid and made the full glasses sparkle like rubies. Jeremy picked up his glass to salute Anne and she followed suit. The sunlight through the wine cast a crimson glow along the fair skin of Anne's wrist.

They sipped wine and nibbled on bread and cheese and fruit as the golden water tumbled over the rocks beside them. A combination of the wine and the warm sunlight on her face and shoulders began to make Anne feel light-headed and sleepy. Jeremy talked of this and that and nothing in particular, and his deep voice surrounded Anne like music. She let his words slide off her ears without making a clear impression until her eyes were half lidded and she rested her chin in her hand.

"Are there any men in your life, Anne?" Jeremy asked abruptly. Anne had only been half listening, and the question caught her off guard.

"There have been."

"I have the feeling that means there aren't now."

"Not in Paradise."

"Were you married?"

"No, thank goodness. It never got that far."

"What happened?"

Anne didn't want to talk about her past affairs, but since Jeremy had talked so openly about his marriage and divorce, she almost felt as if she should.

"Nothing, really. Rick always assumed that I was a complete idiot, and everything had to be his way. Whenever I tried to talk about quitting my job and starting my shop, he just laughed as if it were the funniest idea he'd ever heard. And when I talked about coming to Paradise, he would just say it was impossible because his job was in Detroit and that was all there was to it. One day I realized that I wanted to move to Paradise more than I wanted to see Rick. I think he was truly shocked when I actually made the decision and moved away. He didn't think I had the willpower."

"And he was wrong," Jeremy added.

"You'd better believe it. He never really believed I was going to do it, even when I started packing. He'd come over to my place and talk about what we were going to be doing next week and next month, after I would have left. Even later, up here, I got a letter every week for the first month or so, ordering me to give up this foolishness and come back. The letters finally stopped coming, so I suspect he's found himself another poor little fool to dominate."

"He never came up here himself?"

"No. That would have been too much trouble. Rick likes things nice and simple."

"That's what makes him a fool. If it were me, I'd have come up here and gotten you myself."

"It wouldn't have done you any good," Anne replied firmly. "I'm determined to have my own life. I am not going to be dominated."

Jeremy's eyes held a silent challenge as she said the words, and Anne felt as if she'd spoken her own epitaph.

"You mustn't confuse me with your old boyfriend," Jeremy replied. "I'd never make the mistake of thinking that you're an idiot. Quite the contrary. I have no interest in idiots. I think you're a talented artist and a reasonably shrewd, if inexperienced, businesswoman. With my help, your business will be successful. We have a lot in common, Anne."

"Is that why you gave me the check? Because you think I can't make a success of my shop without your help?" Anne felt her anger rising. Just like Rick and her old boss, Mr. Masters, Jeremy was assuming that she couldn't survive without male guidance.

"Don't get upset," Jeremy replied smoothly. "A quick look around your shop showed me that you were undercapitalized. But you did a wonderful job with what you had. You could make a success of the place on your own if you had the time to build a clientele. But without adequate capital you don't have that time. That's the reason most small businesses fail in the first year. It isn't any failing on your part. That's just the way it is."

Anne stared intently into her now-empty wineglass. "I don't want to be indebted to you or to anyone else."

"You're not. That check wasn't a loan. It was advance payment for three windows. You don't owe me anything but windows. But I really didn't come out here to discuss business," he said with an inviting smile. Anne tried to avoid his eyes but found she couldn't. His smile was like a magnet that drew her eyes to his face. When she looked at his thick, arched eyebrows, sparkling dark eyes, and bushy mustache, she couldn't help but smile back. Jeremy leaned over to kiss her lightly on the lips, and the touch raised a blush on her cheeks.

Jeremy chuckled. "My, my, you blush easily." Anne blushed all the more deeply in response and Jeremy just laughed as she turned progressively deeper shades of red.

"I thought you weren't going to make any passes," Anne said.

"I said I wouldn't make any passes that you weren't receptive to. I don't notice any kicking or screaming."

Anne started to gather up the remains of the picnic, if only to have something to do with her hands. She wrapped the wineglasses in napkins and put them back in the knapsack. Jeremy gathered up the bread crumbs and the remaining cheese and wrapped them as Anne folded the tablecloth. When everything was neatly packed away, they both stood up to brush the crumbs off their clothes. Jeremy carried the knapsack by the straps and put his free arm around her waist as they walked slowly along the path, leaning closely together, savoring the beauty of the woods and the closeness of each other's body. The only sounds were the dry rattle of the leaves beneath their feet, the calling birds, and the faint rushing of water in the distance.

Shortly, they came upon a spot where the leaves had drifted deeply against a rock outcropping near the path. Jeremy stopped, set down the pack, and picked up a handful of leaves. He had a mischievous twinkle in his eyes.

"What are you going to do with those?" Anne asked.

"Make you the queen of the autumn forest," he said

playfully. He held the handful of dry leaves over her head, sprinkling them over her hair and shoulders. A leaf tickled her nose as it drifted down to lodge in the neck of her shirt. Anne shook her head to free her hair of leaves and picked up a handful of her own.

"In that case, I'm going to make you into the stuffed shirt of the autumn forest." She quickly tucked a bunch of leaves down the front of his shirt.

"Uh-oh, you're asking for it." Jeremy laughed as he pulled out his shirttail to free the leaves. He picked up a double armload of leaves and threw them at Anne, who fell to her knees and churned a cloud of dry leaves into the air around Jeremy. Before the leaves could settle, he had dropped to his knees directly in front of her and surrounded her in a strong embrace. The flurry of yellow and red leaves settled around them, covering them to their waists as Jeremy's lips pressed against Anne's. He kissed her cheeks and eyelids and the warm hollow of her neck below her chin. A shudder of pleasure ran through Anne's body as Jeremy drew a line from the base of her neck to her chin with the tip of his tongue. She returned his kisses with abandon and buried her fingers in his dark curly hair. Ever so gently, he lowered her until she rested on her back in the soft bed of leaves. His face hovered above hers as she reached up to caress his muscular neck.

"Now, my love," Jeremy said in a soft, mocking tone, "all you have to do is tell me to stop, and I won't lay another hand on you. Shall I stop?"

His gentle teasing excited Anne all the more and her blood seemed to burn as it coursed through her veins. Her heart pounded as if it would escape from her chest and fly away.

"No," she sighed. "Don't stop." With that, Jeremy's mouth descended to smother hers with a kiss as he slowly opened the buttons of her flannel shirt, one by one, spreading apart the soft material to expose the silky white skin of her chest. He lifted her gently with one arm while he slipped the limp shirt off her shoulder with the other. She lay back, naked and exposed to the waist. Jeremy sat up and moved to straddle her prone body. He gazed adoringly at her pale white skin and the small mounds of her breasts. Anne trembled in anticipation of his touch. Then it came. His soft, smooth fingers traced swirls around her breasts, then slowly climbed the mounts to find the hard pinnacles of her rosy nipples. He leaned over and took each nipple in his mouth in turn, flicking his tongue over the sensitive, excited skin and sucking gently. Anne's fingers dug into the rough material of his blue-jeaned thighs and a breathy exclamation of delight escaped her mouth.

"Sh," Jeremy said as he suddenly but gently placed a hand over Anne's mouth and lay down to cover her body with his. At first she couldn't imagine what he was doing, but then she heard the approaching footfalls on the path. She lay completely still, almost fearing to breathe. Without moving her head, Anne could just see an elderly couple, with their small Pekingese dog on a long lead, walking leisurely down the footpath from the falls. The old couple seemed entirely wrapped up in each other. They didn't look to either side of the path as they walked. The man had his arm around the woman's waist and the little dog scampered here and there to either side of the path as they went. They were having a quiet conversation, and Anne could hear the low buzz of their voices but couldn't make out any words.

Far from dousing her ardor, the sudden danger of discovery had the opposite effect on Anne. She wondered at herself as the delicious sense of danger spread through her body in waves of tingling, almost unbearable pleasure. Her heart raced and when she dared to take a breath, it came in a ragged gasp. The little dog trotted off the path when the couple got close enough, and it sniffed at Jeremy's shoulder. Anne could feel the warm puffs of its breath as it looked at her, and she had to hold her breath to keep from laughing as the little squashed face came closer. The couple passed by without noticing Jeremy and Anne, half buried in the leaves as they were, and when the leash went taut as they reached its limit, the old man gave the little dog a sharp tug.

"C-c-c-come on, P-P-P-Pookie," he stuttered. Anne was convulsed with a silent giggle as she heard the man's stutter. Jeremy kept his hand over her mouth to keep her quiet.

"Sh," he whispered. "They'll hear you."

Anne laughed as he removed his hand. "I don't care if they do." They were far enough down the path by now to make it safe.

"Shameless hussy." Jeremy laughed. Anne was surprised to see that he had turned beet red when he finally sat up. Anne was embarrassed, but not *that* embarrassed. She could see that the danger of discovery had bothered Jeremy much more than it had her.

"Now *you're* blushing." She giggled, the incident seeming wonderfully funny to her now.

Jeremy slipped the shirt back up over her arms and started to button it, then chuckled. "You know, we're both old enough to know better than this."

"I'm just relieved that P-P-P-Pookie didn't p-p-p-piddle on us," Anne said and laughed.

Chapter Four

When they arrived back at his house, Anne was still enjoying the look of embarrassment she had seen on Jeremy's face. The sun had almost disappeared behind the hill, and long shadows of trees were creeping up the west wall of the house. The sky had turned a brilliant magenta and the small, wispy clouds were outlined in fiery gold.

"I arranged this display for your benefit," Jeremy said with a smile as he opened her door. He gestured at the colorful sky framing the dark house.

Anne laughed. "Then I have to compliment you. You must be something of an artist yourself."

Jeremy offered his hand to help Anne from the Blazer. They walked around to the front of the truck and Jeremy put an arm around her shoulders as they leaned back on the hood to watch the impressive light show in the sky.

"I had a wonderful time this afternoon," Anne said quietly.

"Don't talk as if it were all over," Jeremy replied.

"I'd better be getting home now."

"I wish you would stay."

Anne paused, not knowing what to say. She wanted to stay; she wanted the beautiful afternoon to go on forever. But something else was telling her that it was time to go—maybe even past time to go. Part of

her mind was warning her that if she didn't break
away now, it would be too late.

Jeremy drew her close and kissed her gently on the
lips. Again, his touch awakened the sleeping woman
within her. The warning voice went unheeded and
Anne knew that she would stay. She'd stay and find
the answers to the questions that Jeremy's touch
seemed to ask.

Together, they went into the empty house. The workmen were gone, leaving behind their incomplete work;
there were stacks of lumber and plasterboard in the
entry hall, paint cans stashed in corners, a roll of
carpet blocked the entrance to the library, and a thin
film of plaster dust seemed to cover everything. Yet,
even as they stood in the midst of the chaos of the
remodeling work, Anne could sense order emerging
from the mess. She could see Jeremy's plans and personality taking hold of the old house and molding it into
something new—something that was part of himself.

"It's going to be beautiful when you get it done,"
Anne said quietly.

"It's already beautiful," Jeremy said. "The changes
I'm making are just on the surface. Josiah laid the
foundations and made this a home. My grandfather
was the caretaker who made sure that home survived,
and now I'm bringing it back to life. It's going to be
something different from what Josiah built, but it's
still going to be a continuation of his dream."

"I find it hard to imagine Josiah dreaming of a
country inn," Anne replied.

"Not an inn, exactly. But he dreamed that there
would always be Brecks living on this hill and that
they would be comfortable and happy and secure.
That was what Josiah's empire building was all about."

"Not a bad dream," Anne said quietly. "I'm not
sure that there's any dream better."

"There isn't."

Anne looked at Jeremy as he stood facing her in the dusky shadows of the hall. In the dim light his craggy features seemed to soften. For a moment he appeared younger—a boy, wearing a false mustache as a disguise. Then, as Anne watched, his face broke into a smile and the illusion melted away into the solid maturity of his muscular neck and shoulders and the confident gleam of his eye.

The entry hall was chilly. The new furnace wasn't working yet and the temporary library windows were still unfinished. The sun had nearly completed its descent behind the hill, and the warm afternoon was turning into a crisp evening. Anne shivered slightly.

"I left instructions for the housekeeper to light a fire upstairs before she went home. It will be warmer in my room," Jeremy said.

"I didn't know you had a housekeeper."

"Hired her this morning. Mrs. Harkness. She seems like a solid, dependable lady. She won't have too much to do until we open up in the spring, but I thought it would be a good idea to let her get used to the place through the winter." Jeremy talked about his new employee in a casual, offhand manner, as if he were discussing administrative details of little importance with a business partner.

He took Anne's hand and led the way up the stairs to his room, where a warm fire crackled in the fireplace. The room was a homey oasis in the chaos of remodeling in the rest of the house. It was neat, clean, and comfortably furnished. Jeremy had taken pains to make this one room livable long before the rest of the house would be ready.

The four-poster bed was covered with a patchwork quilt. An oval braided rug covered the polished plank floor on either side of the bed, and beige antique-satin curtains hung at the windows. The wallpaper was a restful vertical pinstripe design, probably original, though still in quite good condition. A large mirror hung over the fireplace and several framed photographs sat on the mantel. A large, overstuffed chair with a padded footstool faced the fire.

Anne walked to the mantel and examined the photographs. They were mostly run-of-the-mill family snapshots. She recognized a younger Jeremy posing with people who, she assumed, must be his parents. His mother was a striking redhead with a free, challenging air. His father was a conventional-looking, though handsome man with Jeremy's sturdy build, but none of his charisma.

There was one photo, however, that was obviously an antique. It showed a middle-aged man, with a huge handlebar mustache, dressed in the style of the 1920s and with a riding crop tucked under his arm. The man had a humorous gleam in his eye and a supremely confident air.

"Josiah?" Anne asked, indicating the picture.

"Heavens, no." Jeremy laughed. "Josiah was long dead before that picture was taken. That's Morton, my grandfather."

Anne compared the picture to one of those she assumed to be of Jeremy's father. She could see a family resemblance between Jeremy and his grandfather, but the father seemed strangely out of place, with his clean-shaven face and almost humble expression.

"I believe it skipped a generation," Anne commented.

"What?"

"Whatever it is about you," Anne replied.

"You might be right. Dad never had any interest in coming back here. I think he was uncomfortable around Grandfather. He felt intimidated, but it was different for me. I guess it's easier being a grandson than a son."

"I bet you were never in any danger of being overshadowed. It would take more than a man to intimidate you."

"I'll take that as a compliment," Jeremy said with a twinkle in his eye. He paused and regarded Anne with a steady gaze. "Now, I promise you, there are no little dogs, meandering retirees, or other interruptions wandering through this house. We're alone." His face took on a serious expression as he stepped closer and looked deeply into Anne's eyes.

"Tell me, Anne, shall we send out for a distraction, or is this our moment of truth?" His hand traced the curve of her cheek and came to rest in the warm hollow of her neck. Anne stepped closer to rest her cheek against his solid chest. She breathed in his heady masculine scent and sighed almost against her will as the unasked-for feelings again rose within her.

"You have to ask?" she breathed, raising her face to greet his waiting mouth.

His kiss enveloped her. As she pressed herself against his chest she felt his heart quicken and her own heart responded in kind.

Suddenly Jeremy swept Anne from her feet. Her head spun as he carried her across the room to set her lightly on the bed. Anne slipped her feet out of her shoes and dropped them over the edge, then she waited, filled with expectation as Jeremy paused to look at her, drinking in every inch of her.

As he watched, Anne slowly opened the buttons of her shirt. She let the soft material fall limply open and met Jeremy's eyes with a steady gaze of her own.

Jeremy's hand slid the shirt off her shoulders and Anne shivered with pleasure at his touch. He loomed over her, his breath warm on her face, his hand lingering on her shoulder.

His mouth came down to meet hers and his kisses penetrated to the very depths of her being. His warm, moist lips made teasing explorations of her face and neck. Anne responded with explorations of her own as her hands outlined the muscles of his back and

enjoyed the springy curliness of the hair on the back
of his head. She moaned in sudden ecstasy as his
teeth found the delightfully sensitive lobe of her ear.

Jeremy sat up and turned his attention to her now
fully exposed breasts. His fingers smoothed over the
gentle rounds and circled the erect, hardened sum-
mits of her nipples. Anne's chest rose and fell as she
struggled to draw air into her lungs. His touch seemed
to rob her of the ability to draw a normal breath, and
a delicate flush spread over her neck and chest. Her
muscles seemed to take on a life of their own as her
back arched to meet his touch and her skin drank in
and savored the smooth tips of his fingers.

She reached out to open the buttons of Jeremy's
shirt and he lifted her from the bed and brought her
face to the warm surface of his chest. As Anne sprin-
kled him with moist kisses, flicking her tongue around
his nipples, the curly chest hairs tickled her cheeks.

Jeremy released Anne from his embrace and leaned
back on the bed. His eyes were glazed with desire and
his chest rose and fell in a rhythm of passion.

As Anne looked at him she could see the power
coiled within his body. He was like a tensed spring,
ready to burst forth at any moment. His skin was
glazed with a thin film of perspiration, shining beneath the dark hairs like burnished metal. Each mus-
cle stood out in bold relief against the others and
Anne watched with fascination as they shifted and
opposed one another beneath his skin.

She had never looked at a man this way. She hungered to unite with the power she saw there—to merge
her body with his and drink at the wellspring of
strength that flowed within.

"You're a witch," Jeremy said in a husky, passion-
laden voice. "I would never have believed that any
woman could do this to me."

Anne stepped off the edge of the bed and opened

the snap at the waist of her jeans. She lowered the zipper and let the garment fall to the floor. Jeremy's eyes wandered the length of her body, then came to rest at the silken triangle between her legs. He reached out and pulled her back onto the bed, crushing her to him and running his hands over the soft curves of her back, buttocks, and thighs. Anne trembled in anticipation of the ecstasy to come.

Then, when she thought she could wait no longer, Jeremy released her and began to unfasten the waist of his own jeans. His wonderful, capable hands were suddenly clumsy, as if they had forgotten how to perform such a simple function. Anne controlled the trembling of her own hands and reached up to perform the task for him. When the encumbering garment was out of the way, he knelt over her, caressing the exquisitely sensitive insides of her thighs and ever so slowly working his fingers toward the aching core of her passion.

Anne's body responded with a delightful agony. She hungered for the final embrace that would release all that was imprisoned within her. "Please, Jeremy, now," she moaned, and in response, Jeremy came to her. There was a moment of sweet pain, then a feeling of wholeness that she'd never before experienced. Fire circulated in her veins and her back arched to meet the rhythm of Jeremy's body. She lost track of everything except the hard length of his body pressed against hers and the building urgency within her. She heard a moan from somewhere far away and realized that it was her own voice, detached from her and crying out of its own accord.

Then, in a moment that nothing in her life had prepared her to expect, the prison doors burst open and all that was within her escaped like a blinding flash of light. For a moment suspended in time, Anne felt as if she had ceased to exist as a separate person and had become one with the fire in Jeremy.

Anne wasn't sure how long they lay clasped together, spent and exhausted. Time had lost all meaning. The tension had gone out of Jeremy's body and now it was warm and comforting—fitting perfectly against every curve of her own. Anne ran her fingers through Jeremy's damp hair and marveled at the wonderful, secure feeling of his closeness. She was amazed by the intensity of what she had just experienced, and even more amazed by her own behavior. She had never imagined herself acting with such abandon. What little sexual attraction there had been between her and Rick had been a cool, dispassionate feeling almost growing out of the conviction that she ought to be feeling something. Never before had Anne found herself in the grip of such an overwhelming desire.

Jeremy rolled over onto his side and propped his head up on his hand. He regarded her with a look of bewilderment. "You were a virgin," he said quietly in a voice that betrayed uneasiness.

"Mmm," Anne replied, trying to hide the awkwardness she suddenly felt.

"You didn't act . . . I mean I wouldn't have guessed."

"I suppose we're back to 'shameless hussy' now," Anne said peevishly.

"No. I didn't mean that, Anne. I was just surprised." He reached out and brushed a lock of fine, curly hair out of Anne's face. His touch was tender and she felt a little ashamed at having taken offense so easily.

"You can just chalk it up to your fantastic prowess," Anne said lightly, making an attempt at humor but knowing that it fell flat. She wondered why she felt so awkward now, when just moments ago she had felt so secure and comfortable.

"I chalk it up to your deeply passionate nature," Jeremy replied with a mischievous twinkle in his eye.

He brushed his fingers around the curve of her breast and Anne again began to feel the wonderful sensations crying to be released.

But this time she didn't listen. She didn't want to listen. She'd regained the control over herself that she had always valued so highly and she didn't want to relinquish it again, even in exchange for the ecstasy she had just experienced. She was suddenly wary of Jeremy's ability to make her forget herself and give herself over to the primitive drives within.

Anne sat up abruptly and slid off the side of the bed. She was now acutely aware of her nakedness and wanted to cover herself as quickly as possible. Jeremy raised his head and beckoned for her to come back to the bed.

"Hey, where are you going?"

"I think it's about time I went home."

"What's the rush? Is something the matter?"

"No. It's just time to go."

Jeremy sat up and looked at her in complete puzzlement. Anne pulled up her jeans and fastened them and started to look around on the floor for her shoes.

"Quit that and come back here and sit down," Jeremy said. "I want to know what's going on."

Anne stood up and looked at him as steadily as she could. For some reason she didn't want to look at him now, but she did. "Nothing's going on. I had a wonderful time today and now I'm going home like a good girl."

Jeremy looked annoyed. "A hooker makes love, gets her money, and goes home. Nice girls stick around."

Anne flushed furiously. "How *dare* you. Only a man would make love to a woman and then accuse her of being loose because she made love to him." Anne picked up one of her shoes and sat down on the edge of the bed to shove it onto her foot.

"Hey," Jeremy said gently. "I didn't mean that. I

just want to know why you think you have to rush off
so fast. I'd like you to stick around." He picked up her
shirt off the foot of the bed and draped it around her
shoulders.

Anne forced the muscles in her back and shoulders to
relax. She knew that Jeremy didn't mean to hurt her.
She also knew that she was acting strangely. She slipped
her arms into her sleeves and buttoned the shirt.

"Would you feel better if I got dressed, too?" he
added. Anne nodded dumbly. "Okay, I'll get dressed.
But I won't pretend that I understand unless you can
tell me what's wrong."

Anne didn't turn around to look at him as she heard
him get up and step into his pants. She busied herself
with her other shoe. When she got up to look at herself in the mirror, she was horrified at the messy state
of her hair, so she got the brush out of her purse and
began brushing furiously. With the sudden feeling of
being watched, she spun around to see Jeremy put a
hand up and hide a smile. He had his shirt on, though
it was unbuttoned, revealing a narrow strip of chest.

"You've never seen a woman brush her hair before,
I suppose?"

"No, I've seen plenty of women brush their hair.
I've just never seen a woman brush her hair as if she
wished she were bald."

Anne took control of the hand that held the hair-
brush and forced it to do its job slowly; soon her hair
was lying as smoothly as could be expected. Anne's
fine curls tended to frizz somewhat under the best of
circumstances. She put the brush back in her purse
and paused for a moment, looking for a graceful way
to excuse herself.

"Come here and sit down," Jeremy said, gesturing
toward the empty side of the bed. "Outside of that
totally uncalled-for remark a moment ago, I'd like to
know why you're so angry at me."

"I'm not angry."

"But you're acting as if you are."

Anne reluctantly sat down beside Jeremy on the bed. She was beginning to realize that the reason she didn't want to be near him now was her fear that he would touch her again and she would lose all self-control. But it wasn't anything she could explain to Jeremy. How could she tell him that she feared him because she feared her feelings for him would sweep away everything else in her life?

"Look, this was wonderful," Anne said carefully. "But why don't we just leave it at that? Every date has to end sometime."

"That's not an answer, Anne." A dark cloud passed across his face. She could see that he was reaching the end of his patience with her unexplained behavior.

Anne pursed her lips and prepared herself to resist his insistence on an explanation. She told herself that she didn't owe him any explanation; she was responsible for her own actions and had to answer only to herself.

"I'm going now," Anne said firmly, starting to get up.

"Not yet," Jeremy said just as firmly. He took her arm and forced her to sit back down. "It's not in my best interests to let you leave here angry."

"*Your* best interests are *not* what I have in mind at the moment," Anne said furiously. "Unless you intend to keep me a prisoner here, I suggest that you let go of my arm."

"Anne, please, give me a break." Jeremy's voice was gentle again. "A few minutes ago you were fine, but now you're bristling like a porcupine. If I've done something to hurt you, I wish you'd let me know so I can make it right."

Anne forced herself to relax again. She knew she was acting irrationally and that was the last thing she wanted to do.

"You've done nothing to hurt me," Anne said quietly. "Except trying to get me to stay after I think it's time to leave. I'm in control of my fate, and for some reason you can't accept that."

Jeremy's brow furrowed as he looked at Anne. "I've never seen such a woman for running hot and cold," he said suddenly. Then his face and his voice softened. "You scared yourself. That's it, isn't it? Love is nothing to be afraid of, Anne. It's losing it that hurts."

"I think you're confusing love and desire," Anne said calmly. "Many people do. The world is full of people who make life-altering decisions on the basis of physical attraction."

"Is that what you think? Anne, believe me, I'm not just after your body."

"Aren't you? How could you know about anything else? We met less than a week ago. I don't know about you, but it takes me a little longer than that to say I love someone."

"Have you ever loved anyone?"

Anne didn't answer. She knew that she had never loved Rick. But despite her words, she was afraid she couldn't honestly say that she didn't love Jeremy.

"If you've never been in love, how can you know how long it takes to fall in love?"

Anne looked at Jeremy in exasperation. She knew she couldn't win a rational argument with him. "Has it ever occurred to you that trying to apply rational terms to an emotional subject doesn't make much sense?" she said finally.

"My point exactly," Jeremy said with a charming smile. Anne sighed because she knew she had lost this round. "Stay, Anne. I'm not going to hurt you."

"I don't think you're trying to hurt me," Anne said, avoiding Jeremy's eyes and staring into her lap. "I just want to go home and be by myself for a while."

"Because you're confused? Because you don't understand what's happened to you?"

Anne shrugged. "I don't know."

"Stay ... You won't find any answers by running home and locking the door." He put a gentle arm around her shoulders and guided her head to his shoulder. "There is more to love than desire. Let me show you."

The will to leave melted away from Anne; Jeremy's shoulder was so warm and comforting. His mood was totally different now, and for some reason that Anne couldn't completely understand, his mood seemed to flow into her. There was no hunger in his touch now, which was gentle and reassuring. He wasn't trying to arouse her as he stroked her hair and lightly kissed her forehead and eyelids. It was a touch that calmed rather than excited. The tension and resistance flowed out of Anne's muscles and she let Jeremy have the control he sought. It was so easy to give herself over to him. It was resisting him that took so much effort.

As she relaxed and let Jeremy hold her, Anne suddenly realized how tired she was. She wondered if her irrational reactions to Jeremy hadn't been partly a result of that fatigue. After all, he was truly wonderful. What more could she ask for? Why was she trying so hard to lose him? The answers were becoming vague and undefined.

The fire popped loudly and sent a shower of sparks up the chimney. It burned more brightly for a moment, then settled down again.

"Don't go away," Jeremy whispered. He got up and put another log on the fire. Anne slipped her shoes back off and pulled her knees up onto the bed. When he returned, they lay down and settled into a loose embrace. Anne rested her head on Jeremy's shoulder as he draped an arm protectively around her. Anne knew that she was moments away from falling asleep and didn't care.

She let sweet oblivion wash over her.

When Anne woke, early the next morning, her first sensation was the weight of Jeremy's arm on top of her. Then she became aware of the warmth of his shoulder beneath her cheek and the soft, regular sound of his breathing. She was momentarily confused, then remembered where she was.

She got up and parted the curtains to look outside. The lawn and drive were dusted with an overnight frost that sparkled brightly. But the sky was clear and blue, and it promised to be another warm Indian summer day.

She heard Jeremy shift in the bed and turned to face him. He was sitting up and blinking as he looked at her. His face was dark with stubble and his shirt was rumpled. She looked down and realized that she was just as rumpled herself.

"Aha. You *have* a fault," Jeremy said. "You wake up with the disgusting birds."

"Don't get up," Anne said with a smile. "I can let myself out."

"Don't start that again."

Anne laughed. "You have to let me go home and change clothes sometime."

"You can do that when we go down and get your things."

"What?"

Jeremy swung his feet over the edge of the bed and stood up. He stretched and rubbed his face. "Excuse me. I'm not worth a damn before I have my coffee and shave in the morning.

"What's all this about going down to get my things?"

Jeremy looked at her as if the question were nonsense and said nothing.

Anne said suspiciously, "Do you have some strange idea about my moving in here?"

"You're going to have to."

"Oh? Why?"

"You're building a window for me, remember? A very large window. I would think you'd be the first to realize that you're going to have some serious problems getting it from your shop to here."

Anne stopped and thought for a moment. The problem had occurred to her earlier, but she had preferred to cross that bridge when she came to it. She'd made some tentative plans about building a wooden frame to fit in the back of Jeremy's Blazer to transport the window panels, but she hadn't any firm ideas.

"Even if you had a vehicle with a large enough bed to transport a window panel, when the weather turns nasty, you're not going to want to have to drive back and forth all the time."

"I could do the building up here and go back to my shop at night," Anne said tentatively.

"You've never been up here in the winter, have you?"

"What's that got to do with anything?"

"Why do you think that so few of the businesses up here stay open in the winter? It's because getting around is a real problem unless you drive a snowmobile. That's a secondary highway your shop is on. Sometimes it's three or four days after a snowstorm before the plows get out here. Believe me, if it were possible to come and go regularly in the winter, I'd be planning to open year round and feature cross-country skiing when the snow comes."

"Are you saying that we're going to be snowed in here all winter?"

"No, it isn't that bad. But you can never count on being able to leave on any given day if the weather turns bad."

Anne frowned. There just didn't seem to be any nice way to say what she had to say. "I don't want to move in with you."

Jeremy looked impatient and sighed in exasperation. "Why do I have this nagging sense of *déjà vu?*"

"Why are you so surprised that I don't want to live with you after knowing you for less than a week?" Anne said angrily.

"Do you think you could put your temper away for a moment and discuss this like an adult?" Jeremy said sharply.

Anne's temper flared, but she got control of it and steeled herself to win this argument. She was suddenly worried that a wrong move now would lose her not only Jeremy but the window contract as well. And she *had* to have that window—it was her only chance of making a success of her shop.

"You're right," she said calmly but with an edge of cold steel in her voice. "If we can both behave like adults, I'm sure we can work out a solution to this problem. I can see your point. I *am* going to have to spend a lot of time up here to do the window. But, after all, this is going to be a hotel, so I'm sure you can spare me an empty room to live in."

"Why are you so determined to shut me out?"

"Why do you think that you own me just because you contracted for a window?"

Jeremy's eyes lit up with anger. "You're acting like a frightened child, Anne. If that's the way you want it, that's the way you'll get it. I guess I was mistaken about you. I thought you were an independent, self-reliant woman, but you're not. You're an insecure little girl."

Anne choked back the retort that was forming in her throat. She wanted to tell him that he was an arrogant fool for assuming that not wanting to continue to sleep with him revealed some flaw in her character. But she didn't reply. Jeremy was clearly and openly angry with her and she was afraid of what he might do with any further provocation. She satisfied herself by fixing him with an icy stare that was filled with her disdain for his point of view.

"Well, let's get going," Jeremy finally said brusquely.

"There's no reason for you to forgo your morning coffee," Anne said haughtily. "I'm perfectly capable of packing my tools and personal belongings, and bringing them back here. I'll be satisfied if you just have my room ready for me when I come back."

"Have it your own way. Far be it from me to trespass on your independence by helping you move your things," Jeremy snapped.

"I'll be back later," Anne said coldly. She turned on her heel and stalked out of the room. She stomped down the stairs, and as she reached the front door a plump, middle-aged woman was letting herself in. Before Anne could make her way around the woman and get out, Jeremy shouted, "And *don't* expect me to offer to help you carry your things upstairs." The outburst from upstairs was followed by the sound of the bedroom door slamming.

"That's fine with me," Anne shouted back. She stomped through the front door and slammed it.

Mrs. Harkness, the new housekeeper, stood surprised and alone in the entry hall.

"One day I've worked here," she mumbled. "And already there are problems."

Chapter Five

It took several trips in the Volkswagen for Anne to bring the majority of her personal possessions and tools up to the house. When she arrived with the first load, Mrs. Harkness met her at the door.

"I assume you're Anne Keene?" the matronly woman asked.

"Yes, and I'm sorry. I should have stopped before to introduce myself. You're Mrs. Harkness?"

"The same." She gave Anne a suspicious look, as if she wasn't sure whether she was facing fish or fowl. Anne forgave her. She was sure the scene earlier must have been quite unsettling for a woman beginning her second day on the job.

"Mr. Breck says that you're to have the room at the south end of the hall. He also said that you're not to worry about anything that's too large to fit in your little car. He'll bring up the large things later this afternoon."

"Oh? And where is Mr. Breck?"

"He had to go into town on business. He'll be back this afternoon."

Anne was secretly relieved that Jeremy wouldn't be around for a while. She would be able to move around, set up her workshop and room to her liking, and get her bearings without having to worry about running into Jeremy and facing the awkwardness between them. Anne was apprehensive about being around him now.

Mrs. Harkness showed her a small room off the main hall on the first floor, where she could set up her workshop. It had a large western window and thus would catch the best of the afternoon sun. The room smelled of fresh paint, as the painting crew had only just finished their work there. The walls were a clean white and the light coming through the curtainless window filled the room.

Anne spent a busy morning driving back and forth between her shop and the house. She left most of her stained-glass pieces behind, bringing only a few to decorate her new workshop and her bedroom. She hoped that vandalism and theft wouldn't be a problem in an unoccupied building on a secondary road, but she decided that she could come down to the shop and check on the place every few days for as long as the weather permitted.

At lunchtime she went into Paradise and had a hamburger and milk shake at the little restaurant on the shore of Whitefish Bay. The bay waters were a deep, jewellike blue, and the clear sky was dotted with a few white, wispy clouds. It was a beautiful day—the kind of day that had originally convinced Anne that she would come here to live.

However, the beauty of the bay had little effect now. Anne stared out across the water as if it were empty space as she toyed with her french fries and brooded about the months to come. She wished that there had been a way to turn Jeremy down without alienating him, but she knew that would have been impossible. He didn't compromise—with Jeremy it was all or nothing. He had said as much during the picnic at the falls. She remembered his words.

"Once you know what you want, you have to go for it. Hanging back to be safe only keeps what you want out of your grasp," he had said. Jeremy didn't believe in carefully studying all aspects of a situation before acting—he simply acted. Anne could see that their differing philosophies of life would keep them forever at odds. Anne never did anything without considering all the angles and possibilities first. Well, almost anything.

The exception had been going to bed with Jeremy Breck. The events of the previous day and night still baffled Anne; it was like looking back on someone else's actions. It hadn't been the Anne Keene she knew giving herself so willingly to a man she'd recently met. Reviewing the afternoon and evening, Anne tried to find what had made her act so impulsively. The only answer she could find was that Jeremy's enthusiasm and spontaneity were contagious. He could sweep her along on the crest of his own dynamism.

As beautiful as the day and night had been, it was going to make her work for the next three months very difficult. Allowing herself to be swept along had been a monstrous mistake, she mused. That was the great recurring mistake of her life. She was always allowing herself to be swept along—by Mr. Masters, by Rick, and now by Jeremy Breck. Well, it was going to stop. Right now. Never again would she let other people determine the course and shape of her life. She was going to take control and become the author of her own fate.

However, as she reviewed her mistakes of the day before, Anne couldn't help but remember the pleasures as well. Those she couldn't bring herself to regret. She had discovered a wonderful set of possibilities, possibilities she wanted to explore at length—someday. Now just wasn't the time for it; she had important things to accomplish first. But someday . . .

Anne paid her check and returned to the house early in the afternoon. The workmen were there and the downstairs was a beehive of activity. A carpenter was crawling up the staircase on all fours, tapping each step in turn with a rubber mallet, looking for risers that needed replacing. A crew of painters was applying enamel to the woodwork and baseboards, and another group was hanging wallpaper down the hall. The air was full of the sounds of labor and the voices of the workmen.

With most of her tools already put away in her new workshop, Anne decided to avoid the confusion downstairs and start organizing her bedroom. Mrs. Harkness brought her linens for the bed and Anne went to work creating a new home for herself.

She put her heirloom crazy quilt on the bed and arranged her toiletries on the bureau. Mrs. Harkness had seen to cleaning the room before Anne started, so she had no dust and dirt to contend with. She hung several small sun catchers in her window to add a bright personal touch to the otherwise drab room; the wallpaper and floor here weren't in as good shape as those in Jeremy's room. But Anne certainly couldn't fault him for taking the best room for himself. After all, he hadn't planned on having any of the other rooms occupied until spring.

There was a small fireplace as well as a steam radiator. Judging by the ever more infrequent noises coming from the radiator, the furnace installation job was nearly done. Anne hoped that there would be heat before nightfall.

She was on her hands and knees, arranging her shoes in a neat row under the edge of the bed, when she saw Jeremy standing in the door of her room.

"Is there anything from your place that you need me to bring up for you?" he asked in a flat voice.

"Just my worktable," Anne replied, standing up. "Wait a minute and I'll get my purse and keys and we can go get it." She tried to sound bright and enthusiastic about the task.

"That won't be necessary. Just give me the keys and I'll go get it."

"I'd be glad to go along," Anne said. "You might need some help loading it."

"I'm sure I can handle it," he said coldly. His tone of voice pierced her; nothing in his previous behavior had prepared Anne for this aloofness. She wouldn't have guessed that so warm and friendly a man could suddenly turn so cold and indifferent. Anne had expected some awkwardness, but Jeremy's manner was far more than awkward. Anne panicked, wondering how she was going to deal with him now.

She got the keys to the shop out of her purse and handed them to Jeremy. "It's the table on the east end of the shop. I've got it all cleared off," she said lamely.

Jeremy turned and walked away without a word, leaving Anne to puzzle over this new face he was showing. It was nothing like the Jeremy she had been getting to know. His reaction seemed to be all out of proportion to the situation. They had both walked away from the morning tiff angry, but Anne had expected Jeremy to cool down by the afternoon—after all, she had. And if anyone had a right to be angry, it was she.

Anne sat down on the edge of the bed to think. The only explanation for his behavior could be that somehow she had deeply hurt his feelings.

Mrs. Harkness had been working out in the hall during Anne's brief exchange with Jeremy, and now the older woman stepped into the room.

"If you don't mind my poking my nose into your business, you don't suppose you could tell me what that was all about?" the housekeeper asked.

"It's going to be a long, cold winter, Mrs. Harkness."

Mrs. Harkness pursed her lips, annoyed at having her question brushed off so lightly. Suddenly Anne wanted to appease her, realizing that the housekeeper

might be her only ally during the coming winter
months.

"I'm sorry, I didn't mean to be rude," Anne apolo-
gized. "It's just such a ridiculous situation. Here I am,
in the process of moving in with a man who isn't
speaking to me."

"Yes, I gathered that much," Mrs. Harkness replied.
"But what caused the trouble?" The woman sat down
next to Anne on the bed.

Anne tried to think of a way to explain the situation
that wouldn't make her sound fickle or make Jeremy
seem like a womanizer. There just wasn't any delicate
way to describe what had happened.

"I don't know if I can really explain it," Anne said
at last.

"Well, I don't suppose it's really any of my business,"
Mrs. Harkness said gently. "I'm sure you two young
people will work out your differences."

Anne sighed. "I'm here to do a job. I'm going to
build a new stained-glass window for the library—that's
all I'm here for."

The look on Mrs. Harkness's face showed that she
didn't give much credence to Anne's protest. "Very
well, dear," she said, giving Anne a motherly pat on
the knee. Anne could see that she wasn't making any
progress toward convincing Mrs. Harkness that she
had no romantic interest in Jeremy, but at least the
woman was warming to her. That was a step in the
right direction.

Anne was looking out her window sometime later
when Jeremy returned with the table from her shop
and called to one of the workmen to come out and
help him carry it in. Anne didn't go downstairs to
greet him because she felt that he'd just as soon not
see her. Her feeling was confirmed when he immediately got back in the Blazer and left as soon as the
table was inside the house. Mrs. Harkness came back

upstairs as Jeremy's truck pulled away down the drive.

"Mr. Breck is going to have dinner in town tonight," she told Anne. "He asked me to leave you something for dinner before I go home tonight."

"That's all right, Mrs. Harkness. I can whip up something for myself, as long as there's some peanut butter and bread in the kitchen."

"I won't hear of it. Part of my job here is cooking," she said indignantly. "And as long as I'm the cook, nobody's going to eat peanut butter for dinner." For all the indignation of the woman's words, Anne could sense a layer of good humor under the surface.

Anne laughed. "Sorry. I'm used to living alone and I usually just have a snack for dinner."

"Well, that's going to stop right now. You have to take care of yourself. No wonder you're so pale."

"I'm sure that you'll take good care of me," Anne said and smiled.

That evening, Anne found out how large and empty the Breck house could be. As she ate dinner at the kitchen table the emptiness of the house seemed to weigh upon her. She wouldn't have said that she was afraid to be alone in the house, but she was uncomfortably aware of the empty rooms and hallways surrounding her. She returned to her room after eating, but found that she was too restless to either read or go to bed.

After a while she decided to explore the old house while she was alone and there was no danger of coming face to face with Jeremy. She worked her way down the upstairs hall, opening doors and peering into the dusty rooms.

The upstairs bedrooms, other than her own and Jeremy's, were still dirty and begging for renovation. The wallpaper was peeling and in one the floorboards were warped. Anne could see that Jeremy had his work cut out for him if he intended to redo these rooms himself before spring.

At the end of the hall, she found a double doorway that opened onto a wide staircase. The stairwell was festooned with cobwebs and dust, and Anne almost decided to forgo this exploration, everything was so dirty. Curiosity got the better of her, however, and she carefully picked her way up the stairs. She was rewarded for her curiosity.

The third floor was almost entirely occupied by a ballroom. Even though in later years the room had been given over to storage, its first purpose was obvious. A raised platform at one end had once accommodated a small orchestra, and an old piano, partially draped with a dusty sheet, was still there. One wall was covered in gilt-framed floor-to-ceiling mirrors. The glass was filthy and the gold was corroded and flaked away in many places, but the original luxury of the room's furnishings was still evident behind the stacked boxes and dusty trunks. She caught sight of her reflection in the mirrored wall and was startled at first. But as she looked at the misty reflection of the small blond girl in the old mirror she found herself imagining a gala ball given by Josiah Breck in this room.

Ladies in wide hoopskirts would arrive on the arms of elegant gentlemen in high, starched collars. A butler would greet them at the front door and direct them to the stairway. The orchestra would strike up a Strauss waltz and the guests would swirl in clouds of satin skirts and black serge tailcoats.

Anne curtsied to an imaginary gentleman and accepted his gallant offer. She hummed a waltz and began to dance at her imaginary ball, but as she made a graceful turn she caught sight of herself in the mirror again and felt foolish. The phantom gentleman was banished and she stopped to take another look around.

The edges of the room were stacked with boxes and trunks and furniture. Anne was delighted to find a rack of old dresses in one corner. They were antiques, dating from the 1880s or 1890s. Anne wasn't enough of a costume historian to date them any more accurately, but she was delighted with the find. The materials were stiff and brittle with age and the colors were faded, yet they had been beautiful dresses— the best that could be made in their period.

Anne fingered the bodice of a light gray taffeta gown with a net yolk, Victorian high collar, and delicate beading on the bodice front. The long sleeves were puffed at the shoulder and tapered to points at the wrist. The waist was adorned with a bustle and the back closed with a closely spaced row of tiny buttons.

The dress seemed to call to Anne. It was as if a whole era had been distilled into a single piece of clothing. After admiring the gown for several moments, Anne could resist no longer. She stepped out of her slacks and shirt, and gently removed the dress from its hanger. Handling it carefully for fear of tearing the age-weakened material, she slipped it over her head and settled it around her waist. It fit fairly well, though it had been made for a slightly taller woman, as the skirt and sleeves were a bit too long. She couldn't reach back to fasten the buttons, so she let the back stay open as she walked to a mirrored wall to examine herself.

The effect wasn't quite right. Anne puzzled for a moment, then realized that the contemporary curliness of her hair was spoiling the picture. She gathered her hair in a hand and held it up to simulate a Victorian bun.

"Ahem." Anne started as she heard the masculine voice behind her. She spun around to find Jeremy standing at the head of the staircase, and she blushed

violently at having been discovered nosing around
and, worse, trying on the dress. Jeremy's face betrayed
nothing. He might be about to berate her for her
nosiness or to laugh at her childish game of dress-up,
but either way, Anne wished she could sink through
the floor and disappear.

"I-I'm sorry," she stammered. "I don't usually go
poking through other people's possessions." She looked
down at the accusing dress hanging on her body. She
couldn't even take it off now with Jeremy watching.
Anne was painfully aware of the open gap at the back
of the dress, and since Jeremy had been behind her,
she knew he must be, too.

"It seems a little late for regrets," Jeremy said with
a raised eyebrow.

"I don't know what came over me," Anne said,
genuinely contrite.

"I don't suppose Dominique would mind," Jeremy
replied vaguely. "She's beyond that now."

"Who is Dominique?"

"My great-grandmother. That was her dress."

"I'm sorry. I really didn't hurt it. I was careful."

"No harm done," Jeremy said without much interest.
Anne felt that she ought to replace the dress on the
rack, but she couldn't undress in front of Jeremy. He
came into the room and looked around as if Anne
weren't there.

"I'm sorry," Anne repeated. She gathered up her
slacks and shirt, ready to go downstairs and change
into her own clothes.

"So am I," Jeremy said quietly before she could
reach the stairs. Anne stopped and turned to face
him.

"You're sorry?"

"It seems that I don't handle rejection very well."

Anne smiled and tried to show that she was willing

to meet him halfway. "I suppose you haven't had much practice," she said.

Jeremy didn't smile back, but his voice was calm and without its earlier bitterness. "I think we need to start over."

"It does seem as if we got things backward," Anne replied. "I always figured that you were supposed to become friends first, then lovers."

"That's what they always say. But in my experience it generally seems to work out the other way."

"I'm going downstairs to take the dress off," Anne said, changing the subject. "I'll bring it right back up."

"Why don't you save yourself the stair climbing? I'll turn my back." Jeremy turned around and Anne wriggled out of the dress to step back into her slacks. She was buttoning her blouse when she realized that Jeremy had turned around to face the mirrored wall.

"*Hey*. That's not fair," she protested.

"Don't be foolish. I've already seen you."

"I *prefer* my privacy, if you don't mind," Anne said sharply, instantly regretting the edge in her voice. Jeremy was trying to reconcile their differences and she was spoiling it with careless words. Yet she was still annoyed at him for having looked.

"I'd swear you were afraid that I was going to lose control of myself and ravish you on the spot. *Really*, Anne."

Anne sighed. His voice was full of disdain. Apparently the truce was breaking down before it could get started.

"What's done is done. Let's not argue about it," she said with resignation. As she replaced the dress on the rack Jeremy started to rumage around in the boxes and trunks. Anne was leaving again and had gotten as far as the stairs when Jeremy called out to her.

"Come here and look at this," he said. He was in a

corner lifting something out from behind a stack of old chairs. His attitude had suddenly changed. The argument was forgotten, and now his voice was full of the excitement of finding a lost treasure. "I've been wondering where this was," he said. "I never thought of looking up here. I was afraid it was lost for good, but you've done me a good turn tonight by luring me up here. It might have been months before I got around to looking through this stuff."

Anne went over to Jeremy, curious about what object could excite him so. She half expected him to have a strongbox full of money or jewels, but she found him holding up a dusty, gilt-framed portrait. At first she could tell very little about it, but Jeremy found a soft rag and gently wiped the accumulated dirt off the surface.

Anne felt a shock of recognition, even though she'd never seen the woman's face before. The painting was of a man with white muttonchop whiskers and an old woman with black braids streaked with steel gray. Though elderly, the couple seemed to have a strength that belied their age. The man stood behind the woman's chair and he had a possessive hand on her shoulder, but what caused Anne to draw in her breath sharply was the woman's dress. It was the very one she had been wearing moments ago.

Seeing the dress in the painting gave Anne an uneasy feeling of having come loose in time. The picture had an eerie reality—as if it were a window looking in on living people rather than a reflection of the past. The two faces were so strong and lifelike. Anne had the strange feeling that the dress in the painting was real and the one on the rack was the image. Without asking, she knew that she was looking at Josiah Breck and his wife, Dominique.

"Some coincidence, eh?" Jeremy said after a while.
"What?"

"The dress. You just had it on."

"I know. It's almost spooky," Anne said thoughtfully. "But why is this painting up here? I would have expected it to be hanging over the fireplace in the library."

Jeremy chuckled. He propped the painting up on a box and sat down on a nearby trunk to continue looking at it.

"Grandmother undoubtedly put it up here. I always knew that there was a portrait because Josiah wrote about the sitting in his journal, but I never knew where it was. It was probably banished up here long before I was born."

"But why? It's so beautiful."

"It ought to be. Look here." He rubbed clean the lower right-hand corner of the painting. Anne looked closely and felt another thrill of recognition.

"*Thomas Eakins*," she exclaimed. "Jeremy, this is valuable. But Eakins lived and worked in the East. Did they go to Philadelphia to have this portrait made?"

"You should know better by now. That's not the way Josiah worked. He commissioned Eakins to come here and paint the portrait. He came and lived here for almost three months."

"Eakins was one of the best-known portrait painters of the nineteenth century, and Josiah got him to come up here to do a painting?"

"Yes, but if you're up on your art history, you'll realize that Eakins was largely unappreciated until after he was dead. He was just a starving artist when Josiah commissioned him. I guess it shows that Josiah was ahead of his time. He saw 'The Clinic of Dr. Gross' on a trip to Philadelphia and decided that this young artist had a future, so he went to quite a bit of trouble and expense to get Eakins to paint this."

Anne took another look at the picture. At first the

white hair and muttonchops had thrown her off, but now she could see the same resemblance she had observed in the photograph of Jeremy's grandfather. It was vague but unquestionably there. More striking, however, was the resemblance in Dominique—Jeremy had her eyes.

Beautiful as Dominique was, there was something incongruous about her. Anne tried to determine what it was. "Why, she's an *Indian*," she exclaimed a moment later.

"Full-blooded Ojibwa."

"What do you know," Anne said. "Who would have thought that the great Josiah Breck would marry an Indian woman? I'd have expected him to import a princess from Europe."

"To be absolutely accurate, he didn't marry an Indian woman."

"But you just said—"

"They were never married. Haven't you heard the story? I thought everyone around here had."

"No, I guess I haven't been listening to the right gossip."

"Well, it was in the mid-1830s, before Josiah got rich. He came up here as a lumberjack when he was just nineteen. It was wild country then. In those days around here you were either a fur trapper, a lumberman, or an Indian. People still remembered the French and Indian War, and relations between the Ojibwa and the white newcomers were strained at best. But Josiah saw Dominique Talltrees and knew he had to have her. He bought her for three bottles of whiskey and a pack mule."

"Her family sold her?"

"As I understand it, she was in the possession of a group of soldiers at the time."

"But Josiah wouldn't marry her?"

"Well, this portrait was painted in 1891, some fifty-five years later, so you could hardly say he ravaged her and tossed her aside. But she was a 'tainted' woman. Under the circumstances, I guess he figured she wasn't the type you married."

"She was the type you live with for fifty-five years?" Jeremy laughed. "Nobody could call Josiah fickle."

"But why was this portrait hidden away up here?"

"I wasn't around to see it, but I've heard that there was considerable mother-in-law–daughter-in-law friction between Dominique and Grandmother. They were both strong-willed women. Grandfather and Grandmother lived here under the same roof with Josiah and Dominique from the time they were married until the old folks passed away. Grandfather had all the advantages when he was growing up that Josiah had lacked. He was the son of the richest man in the county, and after going away to school at the University of Michigan in the Lower Peninsula, he married the daughter of a wealthy family from Detroit. I'm sure you can imagine how well it sat with Florence when he brought her back here and she found that she was going to be living with an Indian woman, and an unmarried Indian woman at that."

"She sounds like a snob."

"She was, but don't be mistaken. In her own way she was a strong, principled woman. She organized the Methodist Church in Paradise and saw to it that the town had a full-time schoolteacher. She also founded the Paradise Public Library. The town has a lot to thank her for."

"But Florence continually snubbed Dominique, and as soon as the old couple were gone, she hid their portrait away up here, right?"

"Essentially."

"And how did your grandfather feel about the way she treated his parents?"

Jeremy smiled and Anne saw that he enjoyed talking about his ancestors. "Well, I think that Morton always knew that Josiah and Dominique didn't need anyone to protect them. They were strong people. From everything I understand, Dominique and Florence were pretty evenly matched. The only real advantage that Florence had was that she was younger and managed to outlive Dominique."

"It must have been humiliating for Dominique," Anne said seriously. "Bought like a prize cow, kept like a harlot, and despised by her son's wife. The poor woman endured a lot."

"Does that look like the face of a long-suffering slave?" Jeremy asked, pointing at Dominique's picture.

Anne had to admit that the picture showed anything but what she was imagining. Dominique's eyes were clear and proud, her head was held high, and she looked out of the painting with an almost haughty glare.

"She was seventy-eight years old when this picture was painted. She lived to be ninety, and I personally think she enjoyed every minute of her life. Florence couldn't wait for her to die, and the old woman managed to hang on for years."

"It doesn't sound like a very happy household."

"Depends on your point of view. I don't think Florence could have been happy in a peaceful household. She was a fighter, and so was Dominique. Grandmother was always reaching for something else. She was never satisfied with the way things were. She wanted to be in control of everything, but she couldn't be. Grandfather would put up with a certain amount of her foolishness, then he would put his foot down and that would be that. But for all the struggling, I really think they loved each other. That was just the way they were. If you didn't have to struggle for it, it wasn't worth having. They wouldn't have had it any other way."

"You make it sound like family infighting was the national sport around here."

"In a way. But in other ways they hung together. If there was ever an external threat, they closed ranks and fought as a unit. Although Florence complained about Dominique to the high heavens, nobody outside the family dared say a word against Dominique around her—Florence wouldn't stand for it."

Anne became aware of Jeremy's eyes on her and she realized that they had been chatting comfortably for some time. The portrait had provided a distraction that had kept Anne's thoughts off Jeremy, but now she was uncomfortably aware of him again. While they had talked of Josiah and Dominique they hadn't been focusing on each other, but now the spell was broken, and Josiah and Dominique, Morton and Florence, were gone. She was alone with Jeremy Breck and she was aware of his maleness—the slightly spicy scent of his cologne, the power coiled in his muscles, the virility that seemed to surround him like an aura.

"It's late. I'm going downstairs to bed," Anne said self-consciously.

"Sure you wouldn't like some company?"

Anne pursed her lips and paused to choose the right words before she spoke. "Don't you ever turn it off? We were doing so well."

"I don't see any reason to pretend that I don't want you."

"Are we going to have to wind up angry at each other at the end of each day? If so, this is going to be a very awkward winter." Anne controlled her voice carefully, eliminating any sign of anger. She spoke evenly and without emotion. Jeremy responded by controlling his own response.

"It would be a step in the right direction if we could talk about this without becoming angry," he said.

"Good. I hope you understand that this isn't a personal rejection. I really do like you, Jeremy, but I'm here to do a job."

"Are the two mutually exclusive?" he asked calmly.

"I think they are."

Jeremy's face did not betray his feelings, and Anne couldn't tell what he was thinking. "In that case I'll respect your feelings." He stood up and left the room. Anne found herself suddenly alone with the painting and boxes and trunks and cobwebs. To her surprise, she was shaking.

Logically, she seemed to have won this round, but she wondered why she didn't feel victorious.

She looked at Dominique's picture again, wondering at the proud face she saw there. Dominique's skin was deeply lined with age, and the hands folded in her lap were gnarled with arthritis but looked completely relaxed. Anne felt strangely close to the old woman. It was like meeting a friend she had known for years but hadn't seen for a while.

"How did you do it?" she asked aloud. "You never had choices, but you appear in complete control. What's your secret?"

Dominique continued to look out of the painting—calm, clear-eyed, and serene.

Chapter Six

❧

Anne started work early the next morning. She woke long before Jeremy and walked to the bathroom at the other end of the hall for a shower. The boiler installation was complete, so there was plenty of hot water and she took her time, luxuriating in the steaming spray. When she was done, she wrapped herself in her terry bathrobe and slipped her feet into scuffs for the walk back to her room. She wasn't about to be caught in the hall wrapped only in a towel.

But her fears proved unfounded, and she passed down the hall and back to her room without hearing so much as a sound from Jeremy's room.

She started to put on her usual jeans and a work shirt, then stopped. Living by herself for so long, she had lost the habit of dressing to be seen. Since the tourist season was over, she'd become accustomed to being alone. There was no one to see what she wore, so she had paid little attention to what she put on, but now she was going to be around people again.

Not just Jeremy, she thought with a frown. She didn't want to dress up for him, but there would be Mrs. Harkness and the workmen. On the other hand, she planned on getting some work done today, so she didn't really want to dress in anything too nice. She was just tired of wearing jeans and a work shirt every day. Since she was going to be around people again, she wanted to look nice.

After some deliberation Anne settled on a compromise. She put on a pair of dark blue gabardine slacks and a blue-and-red-plaid blouse with a gold thread woven into the design. The cuffs and collar were outlined with a narrow self-fabric ruffle, and the front was closed with a row of delicate pearl buttons.

Anne brushed out her fine blond curls and secured them away from her face with a pair of shiny metal barrettes. Her toilet complete, she examined herself in the vanity mirror, satisfied with what she saw there. The outfit looked crisp and businesslike, and her face had a healthy glow. The work she planned to do today wasn't terribly dirty, so she didn't have to worry about spoiling the clothes, but at the same time, the outfit wasn't so dressy that she would look as if she were dressing up to impress Jeremy. That was the last thing she wanted to do.

Anne went downstairs quietly, careful not to disturb his sleep. It was still quite early, only a few minutes past six o'clock. Rising early had always been her habit. She enjoyed the peacefulness of the hour when most of the world was still sleeping.

Her first stop was the kitchen, where she fixed herself a cup of tea. Cup in hand, she went to her workshop to get started, but before delving into the task at hand, she took a few moments to look out the window at the frost-dusted lawn. The sun had barely cleared the tops of the trees and long, dawn-gray shadows stretched across the lawn. The air was crisp and still, without a breath of wind, and a lone squirrel picked his way across the lawn looking for a buried nut. Anne followed his zigzag course across the grass as he sniffed here and there, dug a little hole, then moved on to a more promising spot. Anne resolved to get some unsalted peanuts on her next trip into town and set them out for the little animal.

Before her tea had time to get cold, she turned

away from the window and prepared to start work. Anne had a small working drawing of the window already prepared, and though it would be several days yet before her special glass order arrived, she had plenty to do until then.

The first order of business was to scale up the drawing to a full-sized diagram of the window. She rolled heavy butcher paper out onto the floor and marked off the dimensions of one of the three panels of the main window. With a yardstick and pencil, she drew the outside frame. Next, using a calculator to scale up her proportions, she blocked out the main features of the window design.

Concentrating on her work, Anne hardly noticed when the workmen started arriving sometime later. She closed her door to shut out the sounds of their voices and footfalls, and continued with her drawing. Before she could go on to the next step, all three panels had to be blocked out this way. She rolled out the second strip of paper and repeated the process for the second panel. She had to make certain that all the lines that crossed over from one panel to the next continued without breaking.

Anne lost track of time. Happy to be working on the window at last, she gave herself totally to the job. The third strip of butcher paper was on the floor and partially blocked out when Mrs. Harkness brought her a bowl of soup and a sandwich for lunch. The housekeeper stood back and admired the huge drawings after she set Anne's lunch on the worktable.

"My, my, nobody could say that you do dainty little sketches," she said.

"I have to work full scale," Anne explained. "After I get all the details laid out on these drawings, I'll cut them apart to make templates to cut the individual pieces of glass. Every piece has to be exactly the right size and shape so that there won't be any gaps."

"I don't know, but that seems like an awful big job for a girl," Mrs. Harkness said in a worried tone of voice.

Anne brushed off her knees as she stood up. "I admit that it's the biggest window I've ever attempted, but I think I can handle it."

"I wouldn't want to try it. Why, just the thought of *washing* a window that size sends shivers down my spine."

Anne took a bite of her sandwich as she walked around to look at her drawings from another angle.

"Oh, no, you don't," Mrs. Harkness said. "You sit down and eat your lunch. You'll ruin your digestion that way." The older woman pulled Anne's stool over to the table where she had laid out Anne's lunch. "You can afford to stop working long enough to eat a meal."

"Yes, ma'am," Anne said humorously. "Can I stay up late tonight, Mom?"

"Now, don't you go laughing at me," Mrs. Harkness said with a frown. "I know what's best."

Anne smiled back at the woman and took a sip of her soup. "Where's Mr. Breck?" she asked, trying to sound casual.

"Upstairs working—and avoiding you."

"Working upstairs doesn't necessarily mean he's avoiding me."

"He doesn't have to try very hard to avoid you when you're hiding."

"I'm not hiding."

"You've been in this room with the door shut since before I got here this morning and haven't so much as stuck your head out the door to say 'Good morning.' If that isn't hiding, I don't know what is."

"I was busy and the noises in the hall are a distraction," Anne protested. "If you'd looked in, I would have said 'Good morning.' "

"You two young people will straighten out your differences a lot faster if you'll talk to each other."

"We are talking to each other," Anne insisted. "As a matter of fact, we had a nice long talk last night. We've both just got our own jobs to do."

"In a pig's eye," Mrs. Harkness replied under her breath.

"Mrs. Harkness, I want to say this in as nice a way as possible. I really don't mean to offend, but has anybody ever called you a busybody?"

The housekeeper laughed out loud. "Honey, I can tell you've never spent the winter up here in the north country. Why, we get all but snowed in for the better part of four months every year. There isn't much of anything to do *but* stick our noses in each other's business. It's practically a national sport up here. If nobody is sticking their nose in your business, it probably means that nobody likes you."

"Well, at least I'm glad to hear that you like me." Anne laughed. "But what makes you think that there's anything going on between me and Mr. Breck?"

"Some things you know from the first moment you set eyes on people. You know what my mother always used to say? 'When people take to door slamming and stairway shouting, it can only mean one of two things: they love each other or they hate each other.' And it doesn't look to me like you two hate each other."

"Your mother must have been something else," Anne said and chuckled, "but there are a lot of feelings between loving and hating."

"Not that go along with door slamming and stairway shouting," Mrs. Harkness said confidently.

Anne polished off her sandwich and handed her plate and bowl to the housekeeper. "Well, all home-spun sayings aside, I think I'd better get back to work. And don't slam the door on your way out," she added with a mischievous wink.

"You can make fun, but you'll see I'm right," Mrs. Harkness said as she left with the empty dishes.

Anne went back to her work and started drawing some of the finer details onto her full-sized diagrams. She tried to keep her mind off Jeremy, but his face kept intruding into anything she tried to visualize. She wondered if he really was staying upstairs to avoid her. It seemed like a childish maneuver, if that was what he was doing. Undoubtedly it was Mrs. Harkness's overactive imagination at work. Jeremy had plenty to do upstairs—there were six bedrooms begging for work, not counting her own. He had explained to her earlier that he was hiring the painting and carpentry crews only for the larger jobs downstairs, intending to repaint, paper, and refinish the upstairs rooms himself.

The afternoon wore on as Anne crawled around on her butcher-paper drawings, adding details, then blocking out the shapes of the individual pieces of glass that would eventually form the design. In mid-afternoon, her back stiff from working on the floor, she took a break, sitting on her work stool with her back absolutely straight to work out the kinks. She was fatigued but satisfied with the progress she was making.

As she rested, Anne became aware of a regular thumping sound from outside. She went to investigate and saw Jeremy in the side yard chopping wood.

The afternoon was sufficiently warm that he was working with his shirt off—and working up a sweat at that. He was concentrating as intently on the ax and log as she had been on her drawings. He wasn't aware that she was watching him, but for all his intense concentration, he was working rather awkwardly. Anne raised the window and stuck her head out.

"I hope you aren't pretending that the log is my head," she said lightly.

Jeremy looked up in surprise and caught the ax

back in mid-chop. He set the head on the ground and leaned on the handle. "Certainly not," he replied just as casually. "But if I were really mad at you, I'd pretend that your head was my hands. I think I'm doing more damage to them than I am to the log." He held out his palms to show the blisters.

"Oh, you're going to ruin those lovely banker's hands," Anne said with mock dismay. "You really should be wearing gloves."

"There's a pair in the hall. Would you bring them out?"

"Sure. Just a minute."

Anne found the gloves at the foot of the stairs and took them out to the side yard. She was glad that Mrs. Harkness had apparently been mistaken about Jeremy's motives for working upstairs. The truce between them seemed delicate, but for the moment it was holding.

"Well, I'm glad that Ms. Trap-door Spider could be lured out of her lair," Jeremy said as he pulled the gloves on.

"Just doing the work you're paying me for," Anne replied.

Jeremy raised an eyebrow.

"Well, if you're going to listen to Mrs. Harkness," Anne said indignantly. "You've been hiding upstairs."

"But I'm not upstairs."

"And I'm not in my workshop."

Jeremy raised the ax and brought it down on the log again, wincing with pain when the shock went through his hands. Anne took the ax from him and propped it up against the chopping block.

"Here, you'd better quit for today or you're really going to hurt yourself."

"I'm afraid that nothing at Harvard Business School prepared me for this," he said sheepishly.

"Well, don't worry. This certainly hasn't tarnished

your masculinity in my eyes. It takes a while for calluses to form. You've got to take it easy at first."

"You sound like an expert."

Anne held up her index finger. "You see that? That's the finger that guides the glass cutter. When I first started cutting glass, I thought I would have to have it amputated. I also took a try at chopping my own wood when I first came up here. Many blisters later, I decided it was worth the money to hire a man to do it."

"I'm glad. I'd hate to think of woodcutter's calluses on those little hands of yours."

"I bet you think I'm too delicate to know how to chop wood. I'll have you know I was an A-one Girl Scout once."

Jeremy shook his head and laughed. "Unfortunately I was never a Boy Scout," he responded.

"If you want some advice, your hands were too close together on the ax handle. And you shouldn't put any force into bringing the ax down. Just let it fall. The weight of the head does the work."

"My, my, aren't you the fountain of knowledge today. Tell me, is there something in the Equal Rights Amendment about equal opportunity to chop wood? If so, I'll gladly turn the job over to you."

"If there had been, it wouldn't have failed. Trust a man to want to turn the hard work over to a woman."

Jeremy stripped off the gloves and took a look at his injured hands. Anne could see that the blisters were pretty nasty.

"Do you have a first-aid kit?" Anne asked. Jeremy nodded in reply. "Where is it?"

"In the kitchen bathroom."

"Let's get some ointment on those blisters." Anne led Jeremy into the house. She was hoping to find Mrs. Harkness in the kitchen so that she could demonstrate that she and Jeremy weren't avoiding each other.

She was rewarded—the housekeeper was peeling pota-
toes at the sink.

Anne tried to act as if she hadn't seen Mrs. Harkness.
She waved Jeremy to a kitchen chair and went into
the bathroom for the first-aid kit. When she came
back out, she concentrated on applying ointment to
the blisters—without looking up to see Jeremy's face
so close to her own or Mrs. Harkness standing a little
farther off. When she sneaked a peek at the housekeeper, she saw that the performance was not unappreciated.

"Thank you, Florence Nightingale," Jeremy said
with a crooked smile. Anne looked up at his face
before she could stop herself. The twinkle in his eye
made her start to blush immediately, and the blush
infuriated her. Why couldn't she look at this man
without changing color? Why did his eyes cut into her
so?

"You're welcome," Anne said evenly. She took out
several bandage strips and covered the wounds.

"It's almost worth hurting myself, if you'll take
care of me," he said teasingly.

Anne's fury mounted. He was spoiling everything.
How could she convince Mrs. Harkness that nothing
was going on if he talked this way? "I'd do as much
for any poor, injured animal," she said coolly. She
snapped the first-aid kit shut and returned it to the
bathroom.

Anne couldn't tell whether Jeremy's expression was
one of resignation or ridicule, but the look he gave her
was odd, to say the least. "Well, in that case, I guess
I'll go back upstairs. He left without another word.

"See?" Anne said, turning to Mrs. Harkness. "We're
talking to each other."

"Oh, I see, all right," Mrs. Harkness said with a
laugh. Anne stalked back to the workshop in frustration.

Inside, she closed the door and leaned against it.

She felt safe here among her tools and drawings. In this room she could tell herself that the only thing that kept her in the house was the window. Outside this room lurked all the dangers and pitfalls that could waylay her on the way to accomplishing her goals. She was hiding now and she knew it; there was no point in denying it.

Through all her frustration, Anne knew she was dead wrong. She had snapped at Jeremy for no reason at all; he hadn't been coming on to her. His comment had simply been a continuation of the friendly mood that she herself had set when she opened the window. She knew that she had lashed out because she was flustered and because she had been trying to show off for Mrs. Harkness. Anne was furious with herself for behaving like a child. Worst of all, she knew that by overreacting she had shown that she *expected* Jeremy to make a pass at her.

Anne couldn't continue to hide in her workshop; that would be the strategy of a frightened child. She couldn't call herself independent unless she could face her problems squarely. If she was going to live in this house and build the windows, she had to be on at least civil, if not friendly, terms with Jeremy. She couldn't go on snapping at him every time he said something pleasant to her. She had to face him as an equal without these outbreaks of self-protective nastiness.

Strengthened by a new determination, she left the workshop and mounted the stairs, feeling as if she were going into enemy territory. By some unwritten agreement her turf had been defined as the downstairs workshop and Jeremy's had become the second floor.

A quick check of the empty bedrooms failed to produce Jeremy. Anne wasn't about to venture into the inner sanctum of his bedroom again. That territory was too dangerous. But before she gave up and returned downstairs, Anne noticed that the door to the ballroom upstairs was ajar.

She found the room as deserted as the second floor had been, but then she noticed a ladder leading up through a trapdoor in the ceiling. She hadn't seen it the night before, but Anne knew immediately that it had to be the access to the cupola that crowned the roof. The trapdoor was open, and she started up the ladder.

Jeremy was sitting on the floor of the little room looking out one of the four windows opening out in each direction. The room was warm and a bit stuffy from the sun shining through the windows. The floor and windows were dusty, and Jeremy's trousers showed smears of dirt from having come in contact with them.

When Anne's head appeared at the trapdoor, he acknowledged her with a small smile. She came up and turned around in the center of the tiny space, taking in each of the compass points through the windows. The cupola was about six feet square and tall enough to stand in comfortably.

From this high vantage point, Anne could see for miles out over the countryside. The orange-and-yellow trees were beginning to look bare, as the majority of their leaves had fallen, but there was still enough color to make the scene breathtaking. As she looked out to the east she was just able to make out the highway and a bit of the roof of her little shop. To the north, gray-blue in the distance, was Lake Superior. To the south and west stretched a seemingly endless sea of treetops.

"I've got to admit that your hiding place is better than mine," she said at last.

"I always used to hide up here when I was little—especially when I was due for a spanking. When I got too big to spank, I still kept coming up here . . . to think."

"I came to apologize. What I said in the kitchen was out of line. I'm sorry."

"It doesn't matter," Jeremy replied vaguely.

"It matters to me. I was rude and there's no excuse for it."

"I was sitting here trying to figure out how anyone who could have been so uninhibited when we were alone could have suddenly turned so terrified of having someone know that I like you."

"I guess I'm just as irrational and flaky as anybody else," Anne said lightly. "Sometimes I don't think of what I should have done until after it's too late."

"I'm not sure which way to take that," Jeremy said. Anne shrugged, unwilling to provide more of an explanation.

"I think I'd like a really big blizzard about now," he said in a faraway voice.

"Anxious to try out your snowshoes?"

"No. I was just thinking about one of the old journals I've been reading. In the winter of 1884 there was a huge blizzard, and nobody could get in or out of Paradise for three weeks. Josiah and Dominique and Morton and Florence were stuck here together for the whole time—couldn't even get out the door."

"They must have been at one another's throats by the time the snow melted, with Florence and Dominique in the same house."

"From what Josiah wrote about it, it was one of the most peaceful times he could remember. There were just the four of them—no outside world, nobody to impress, nothing to work for or against. They had plenty of food in the house and everything just stopped for a while. I guess they had good enough sense to suspend the hostilities as well. I remember one entry from the journal: 'For this time we are just ourselves.

The world beyond these walls is as far away as the Orient. Never before have we seen each other so clearly and without pretense, and I shrink from the day that must come when the snow melts and we must again embrace the outside world and our public selves.' "

Anne sat down at the edge of the trapdoor and let her feet dangle. She gazed out the window, unsure of what her response to Josiah's words should be.

"That's the real problem, you know," Jeremy said after a pause. "We were doing just fine when it was just the two of us, but now there are people around and I have to exercise my male ego, and you have to protect your reputation. It seems that we're working at cross purposes."

"That seems to be the size of it," Anne said quietly. "But I don't think a blizzard is the answer."

"It does seem a little drastic," Jeremy replied with a smile. "But it doesn't really matter at the moment. We won't be making any more scenes for a while."

"How's that?"

"I'm going to be gone for a few days. I'm flying down to Chicago to help Jean out at the bank."

"Oh? I thought you were through with the bank," Anne said uneasily. Something about Jeremy going to Chicago to help Jean made her uncomfortable.

"I am officially, but when I left, I promised to help out if there was an emergency. There's going to be an important vote at the board meeting next Tuesday and it's Jean's first real challenge. If she loses this, she'll never get a secure control of the board, so I want to give her some backup, some support. Let some of the right people know that I'm behind her and all that. She could probably pull it off on her own, but she isn't really confident about it all yet."

"I see. Well, good luck." Anne held her voice absolutely steady. Jealousy was welling up in her, but she didn't dare let the irrational emotion show. She was doing her best not to have any ties to Jeremy, but the feeling was there just the same.

"I'm glad you came up here and we could talk," Jeremy said. He was still looking out the window, and had hardly looked at her since she came up. "I would have hated to leave if we were still mad at each other."

"I don't see that it matters. We can't fight if you're in Chicago."

Jeremy looked directly at her for the first time. "There's nothing wrong with fighting, Anne. It's holding a grudge that's dangerous."

"I'm afraid I come from gentler folk than you. I can see how the Brecks used their fighting spirit to make themselves strong and some of it was left over for bickering among themselves, but in my family we always tried to avoid fighting. There's always the possibility of hurting someone, if you're not sparring with a thick-skinned Breck."

Jeremy laughed. "I guess we are a thick-skinned lot. But you seem to hold your own, for a flatlander."

"Somehow you seem to bring out the worst in me."

"I don't know. Maybe it's the best and you just don't know it."

"Well, have fun in Chicago."

"I'm going to hate every minute of it. I didn't come up here so I could go back to Chicago, but loyalty is loyalty. Oh, by the way, the parcel service called a while ago. One of your glass orders is in. I'll pick it up for you before I go to the airport tomorrow morning."

Anne's eyes lit up. She was getting to the point in her work where she would need some glass to work on. "Did they say where it was from?"

"Germany," Jeremy answered without sounding particularly interested.

"Good. That's the one I was most worried about."

"Well, then, you'll be busy while I'm gone."

"Needless to say."

Jeremy peeled back a bandage on one of his palms and looked at the blister underneath. "By the time I get back I'll be able to take another try at chopping wood. Then I can see if your advice works." His mood seemed to be lifting. He had been uncharacteristically morose since Anne had come to the cupola, but for the first time some of his usual good spirits and humor were starting to show.

"When you get back I should have some glass put together to show you."

"Just be sure to keep yourself in fighting trim," Jeremy said with a smile.

Jeremy stood up and started down the ladder. When he was several steps down, low enough that he was level with Anne, he leaned over and gave her a quick kiss. It was just a friendly peck, lacking in the passion she had come to expect from him, but the touch of his lips caused Anne's heart to leap all the same. Before she knew what had happened, his head disappeared through the trapdoor and he was gone.

Anne stayed in the cupola for a while and thought about all that had happened. Jeremy's kiss left her uneasy. It was too casual and seemed to assume something, but Anne wasn't sure what. Was he taking it for granted that they would be friends now and nothing more? In her quest to meet him equally, had she thrown away her chances at something more valuable than she had realized? Would he stop looking at her as a woman and see her now as a friend and employee?

Anne's feelings were in turmoil. She recognized her jealousy over Jeremy's willingness to run to Jean's rescue, but she wasn't sure what it meant. She told herself over and over again that she didn't want a romantic relationship with Jeremy. It would be to her advantage if he were to rekindle his relationship with Jean. But the idea was distressing.

Deep inside, Anne had to admit that on some level she was already attached to Jeremy. She couldn't just let go, but was it because of the intensity of their first few days together, or was it just his overpowering personal magnetism? She couldn't answer these questions. She just knew that she didn't want him to get away and yet she didn't think she wanted to be committed to a permanent relationship.

"You can't have your cake and eat it too," she said quietly. Her voice sounded strange to her as it filled the small room. She looked out to the north over the distant lake; the sun was sinking low in the western sky, and the light from the window on that side warmed her face. She could see the tiny forms of fishing boats making their way back to the wharf in Paradise after a day's fishing. The water was blue and calm but Anne could see clouds approaching from the north. Indian summer was over. The clouds would bring in cooler weather by morning.

It's an elusive paradise, Anne thought. I've got everything I wanted: my business is going to survive, I'm on my own, I'm independent, and nobody controls me. Why doesn't it feel better?

Chapter Seven

❧

Jeremy was gone for a week. Anne was busy in her workshop from early morning until she lost the light in the late afternoon. She taped the butcher-paper templates to the large flat sheets of colored glass, then cut shape after shape with her Bristol diamond glass cutter. She played little games with herself—finding the least number of cuts she could get away with to define a shape, seeing how close together she could place shapes on a single sheet of glass and cut them without spoiling them.

The stacks of odd shapes—often unrecognizable when out of context—grew on her worktable. Each tree on the stained-glass hill was formed out of two shades of green glass with a smoke-glass trunk. The pieces that made up the sky varied from a turquoise blue to a rosy pink. Anne cut opaque white swirls for the upper sides of the clouds and ruby for the undersides. Before Jeremy returned, the other two shipments of glass arrived and she had most of the glass for the main window cut and was starting to solder together the pieces for the first panel.

The work was going more quickly than she had expected, partially because the main window called for larger, but not necessarily more, pieces than her smaller works, but also because she was blocking out her confused feelings for Jeremy by really concentrating on her work.

Indian summer gave way to the bracing temperatures of autumn, and the bright fall leaves passed through their moment of glory and piled in drifts on the ground. The treetops looked bare and forlorn as their proud fall garments blew away in the lightest breeze.

The carpet layers, painters, and plumbers completed most of their work on the third day after Jeremy left; Mrs. Harkness's kitchen had its new floor and fixtures, the carpet was laid in the hall and up the stairs, the downstairs walls were painted and wallpapered, and the furnace was in full operation. The electrician called to say he had the flu, which would delay the remainder of his wiring for a week or two.

The house was warm in contrast to the chilly outdoors, and the downstairs seemed to be continually filled with the delicious fragrances of Mrs. Harkness's baking. At first Anne wondered who Mrs. Harkness could possibly be baking for, since they had the house to themselves, but a few days later she found out that the housekeeper was baking pies and bread that were sold in a small market in Paradise. Mrs. Harkness and Jeremy had worked out the plan together. The baked goods were sold under the Paradise Inn label and Mrs. Harkness kept the profits in return for her work. Anne had to admit that it was a clever promotional angle. Jeremy got free advertising every time someone bought one of Mrs. Harkness's pies, and Mrs. Harkness was picking up some extra money.

With the crews of carpenters, plumbers, and painters gone, the quiet that settled over the house began to weigh on Anne. She took to playing a portable radio in her workshop to break the silence. Mrs. Harkness would come in and observe whatever Anne was doing from time to time, making small talk, admiring a particular piece of glass, or bringing Anne a snack or a cup of coffee. But most of the time Anne was alone. She felt more solitary now than she ever had in her shop, possibly because the shop had been her home, and this place belonged to someone else.

But Anne also knew that it was because she missed Jeremy. In the short time she'd known him, he had almost always been around her; one way or another, he had been the center of her existence since the moment they met. She hadn't realized that she could have become so accustomed to having someone around in such a short time, but even though they had rarely spoken to each other, Anne was now constantly aware that he wasn't home. She kept wanting to show him her progress on the window. Come to think of it, he had never even seen her drawings. Now that she was actually assembling glass, she wanted him to see her work and either approve it or tell her what was wrong. In her heart Anne knew what she had done was right. It was possibly the best work she had ever done, but she wanted Jeremy to see it and say so.

Anne took one afternoon away from her work for a special project. She went up to the old ballroom and brought down the painting of Dominique and Josiah, sure that Jeremy wouldn't mind. After several hours of carefully cleaning the frame and the surface of the painting, she took it into the study and hung it over the great fireplace.

The portrait obviously belonged there. When she hung it, Anne imagined that Josiah and Dominique looked relieved to be back in their rightful place in the house.

The Tuesday of Jeremy's board meeting came and went, as did Wednesday. Anne had expected Jeremy to return as soon as the meeting was over, but she and Mrs. Harkness heard nothing from Chicago.

The delay in Jeremy's return did nothing but con-

vince Anne that Jeremy had reconciled with his ex-
wife. After all, it was only reasonable. Jean was
obviously the perfect woman for Jeremy. She had to
be intelligent if Jeremy believed her capable of running a huge, metropolitan bank, and she had to be
beautiful, too—Jeremy would never have married her
otherwise, even if her father *was* a chairman of the
board. She was sweet and easy to get along with—he
had said as much during their picnic. The only stum-
bling block Anne could see was that Jeremy had clearly
said that he didn't love her, but that could always
change. Anne imagined the scene: sweet, beautiful,
wealthy, Jean greeting Jeremy at the airport, overcome with relief that he had come to help her, need-
ing him as she never had before.

The scene became an obsession with Anne, to the
point where she revised it in her imagination again
and again. It always ended the same way: Jeremy
promised never to leave Jean again and sent word to
close the house in Paradise. He would be ever so
gallant about it, insisting on paying Anne the full
amount agreed on for the windows, even though they
would never be completed.

On Thursday afternoon, as Anne sat in her workshop and carefully fitted a piece of lead came around a
piece of emerald-green glass that would soon be the
sunny side of a pine tree, she happened to glance out
the window.

"Mrs. Harkness," she called out. "Come look. It's
snowing."

Mrs. Harkness came into the room, wiping her hands
on her apron. "I know you're from southern Michigan,"
she said humorously, "but I would've expected that
you'd seen snow before."

"But not here. This is officially my first Upper
Peninsula snow. It's beautiful—I love it."

"Tell me that five years from now." Mrs. Harkness laughed. "I've seen so much Upper Peninsula snow in my life that I don't care if I ever see another flake."

"Oh, I don't believe that. If you really hated snow, you'd move to Florida."

"You're probably right. Joe and I have talked about retiring south, but I know it wouldn't be long before I started to miss the white stuff. You know, it's really beautiful when the snow is new. It's so clean. I always think about sheets when you first put them on the bed, or great piles of white swansdown."

"I think about clouds. Fluffy white clouds on a sunny day."

"When I was little, we used to rush out and collect the first snow and mix it with sugar and milk to make snow cream."

"Really? Was it good?" Anne asked.

"Not really. But it was special because it was the first snow."

"It's only the beginning of November," Anne said suddenly. "Are we going to be socked in all winter?"

"It may thaw two or three times yet before winter really gets here," the housekeeper replied. "When winter is here, you'll know it. Why, this is hardly enough snow to look at. We don't even start calling it snow until it gets up to your waist."

Anne laughed. "If I didn't know better, I'd say I was getting a snow job."

"*Snow job*. Wait till the old geezers in town tell you about the time it snowed so deep that it didn't melt until July."

"Is that true?"

"If you'll believe that, I've got some real estate in Lake Superior I'd like to sell you."

"Do you think they'll close the airport?" Anne asked.

"I doubt it. Worried about when Mr. Breck will come back?"

"It doesn't matter. I just hate to think about him getting stuck somewhere."

Mrs. Harkness chuckled knowingly. "Well, I wish he'd at least call and tell us when he's coming back."

"I'm sure we'll hear from him when he finishes his business," Anne said evenly.

"Probably," the housekeeper replied. She excused herself and went back to the kitchen, where she had been busy wrapping the latest products of her oven. Anne continued to look out the window at the gently falling snow. There was almost no wind, and the flakes drifted lazily down, some sticking to the window and melting into tiny crystal droplets. The lawn was dusted with it, and the big wet flakes were starting to stick to the windowsill.

Now Anne found it difficult to concentrate on her work; she just wanted to stare out the window at the clean white flakes drifting down. The snow continued to fall throughout the afternoon, and by dusk there were two or three inches on the ground.

She ate her supper in the kitchen after Mrs. Harkness went home, thinking sadly about Jeremy's absence. When she had finished and washed her dishes in the sink, Anne decided she needed something to cheer herself up. With that in mind, she dressed warmly in two pairs of socks, boots, a sweater, her heavy jacket, and a knit hat and scarf, then went outside to experience the snow firsthand. She switched on the porch light and walked out onto the smooth white lawn, turning around and looking up into the sky as the snow tickled her face. It was perfect packing snow. Anne reached down to make a snowball and threw it as far as she could.

Anne's fondest winter memory came back to her then. At the first deep snow her father would always

call to her to come out and help build the snowman.
One year she and her dad had outdone themselves.
After a blizzard that closed school and kept her father
home from work, they built a snowman so tall that a
photographer from the local newspaper had come and
taken a picture that ran on the front page. She still
had that picture in a scrapbook at the bottom of one of
her dresser drawers.

Anne picked up a double handful of snow and packed
it into a large ball that continued to grow as she rolled
it around the yard. The porch light provided enough
illumination for her to work around most of the front
lawn. The air was bracingly cold and her breath formed
white clouds in front of her face. Soon she had a ball
about three feet in diameter and was ready to start
the snowman's midsection.

She was struggling to roll the second ball up onto
the first when she heard the car coming up the drive.
As the headlights topped the hill she saw that they were
too high off the ground to be anything but Jeremy's
Blazer. He was back.

Her first impulse was to run up and meet him at
the door of the car, but she quashed that. She continued to push the big snowball as if she hadn't seen
anything while Jeremy approached. His footfalls were
muffled as he crossed the new snow.

His appearance was markedly different from what
she had expected. She had never seen him dressed for
business before, and his camel-colored double-breasted
overcoat and expensive-looking fur hat took her by
surprise. Snowflakes dusted his hat and shoulders
and stuck in his eyebrows and mustache. A few had
melted against his rosy cheeks, leaving behind cold
droplets of water that glistened like teardrops. He
was carrying his suitcase in one hand and his brief-
case in the other, but as he walked over to watch

Anne's efforts with the snowball, he set down his burdens in the snow.

"You look as though you could use some help," he said with a casual smile.

"Well, don't just stand there—*push*," Anne replied lightly.

Jeremy came around and applied the necessary extra force to rock the ball up into place. It wasn't until the task was complete that Anne started to feel foolish about what she had been doing. Last week he had caught her trying on the dress in the ballroom; now she was building a snowman—was there any end to the foolish things she would see her do?

"That's a mighty fine snowman you've got started there, ma'am," Jeremy said with a mock Western accent.

Anne giggled in embarrassment. She cast around for a way to change the subject and take Jeremy's attention away from her folly. "Did your meeting turn out all right?" she asked coolly.

"Everything went smoothly. Jean did a fantastic job with her presentation, and after I whispered the right words in the right ears, the vote went down like Sherman through Georgia."

"You certainly took your time getting back."

"Did you miss me?"

Anne shrugged. "Mrs. Harkness was worried about how much grocery shopping to do, since she didn't know when you'd be back."

"Well, I was going to come back earlier, but Jean was so grateful after the board meeting I decided to stay on awhile and keep her company," he said casually.

Anne turned away to hide any emotion on her face as her heart sank. Her worst fears had come true. When she looked back, Jeremy had a curious grin on his face—he looked as if he were about to burst out laughing.

"You really are an easy mark," he finally said. "You'd believe anything, wouldn't you?"

"What do you mean?" Anne said defensively.

"You're so jealous that you're turning green. Well, I'll tell you, Anne. I was dying to get back here. Chicago was dirty, wet, and crowded. O'Hare Airport has been socked in with fog since Tuesday evening and it still is. I couldn't get a flight out, so I rented a car to drive to Detroit and caught a flight out of Metro at noon today."

"You're awful. Why did you tell me such a story?"

Jeremy laughed. "Because subterfuge seems to be the only way to get a genuine reaction out of you."

"I wasn't jealous. I was just worried that if you went back to Jean, you would close up the house and I wouldn't get to finish the windows."

"Is that so?" Jeremy laughed. "If you keep lying that way, your nose is going to grow. Where do you get your crazy ideas? I have a lot invested in this place. Why would you think that a casual visit with my ex-wife would make me give up my plans and go back to Chicago?"

"It seemed reasonable when I thought of it," Anne said lamely. It's useless, she thought. I may as well tell him the truth. "Okay, I was jealous. Satisfied?"

"Oh, yes. Victory has such a sweet flavor."

"Well, don't crow too much over your ill-gotten gains. Remember, time wounds all heels."

"Are you going to finish that snowman, or are we both going to stand here until we freeze?"

"Well, don't just stand there. Find a broom or a carrot or something." Anne laughed, suddenly swept away in a feeling of euphoria, which she didn't stop to analyze. After a week of brooding it felt so good just to let it take hold of her.

"Hold on a minute." Jeremy picked up his suitcase and attaché and went into the house. Anne busied herself making the smaller snowball to form the head. In a surprisingly short time he was back, now wearing jeans, boots, and a down jacket. He had a handful of charcoal briquettes, and a carrot was sticking out of his pocket.

Anne laughed. "I can see you're an expert at this."

"Are you kidding? Nobody builds a snowman as well as I do."

"Did you ever have your snowman on the front page of the *Eastside Weekly*?"

"No, I can't stay that I have."

Jeremy lifted the snowman's head in place and pressed the charcoal in for the eyes and mouth. Anne pulled the carrot from his pocket and put the nose in place.

"Wait a minute," she said, running to the edge of the lawn. She broke a couple of dry branches off a small tree at the edge of the woods and came back to poke them into the middle snowball for the arms.

"Fantastic," Jeremy said. "A true work of art. Too bad it won't last. Weatherman says it's going to be sunny and in the mid-forties tomorrow."

"Oh," Anne said with mock dismay. "Can't we save him? Maybe you could airlift him to Alaska. Better yet, airlift Alaska here."

"Maybe we could build a huge freezer," Jeremy said thoughtfully.

Anne laughed. "I know. A threat of force. 'Dear Sun: Do not melt my snowman—or else.'"

"You're crazy, do you know that?" Jeremy laughed. So suddenly that Anne didn't have a chance to protest, he swept her into his arms and kissed her. His lips were warm, much warmer than her own, and her heart beat wildly as she surrendered herself to the warmth of his embrace. "I missed you," he whispered, his breath tickling her cold ear. "I'd rather be here with you than in Chicago any day of the week—even when you're being unreasonable."

"And I missed you. That house is too big and empty when you're away."

"So, I'm adequate for casual companionship," Jeremy teased, "keeping you from being lonely in that big empty house. I suppose that will have to do if I can't get passionate love."

Anne pouted. "Don't tease me. It's not fair."

"And I suppose you've never teased anybody? I have to protect myself," Jeremy replied with an odd smile. "Tomorrow morning you'll probably hate me again."

"I've *never* hated you."

"No, I know that. Let's go inside and get something warm to drink." Jeremy put his arm around Anne's shoulders and they walked back into the house. He snapped on the entry-hall light and turned off the porch light, then unzipped his jacket. Anne kicked off her boots and walked down to the kitchen in her stocking feet. She found a quart of milk and some cocoa and set about to make hot chocolate.

"I've got to show you what I've done on the window," Anne said as Jeremy came in from the hall.

"That can wait for the morning. It will look better in the light," he replied. He sat down at the kitchen table and watched Anne as she worked around the stove. She was aware of his eyes following her, but for once his scrutiny failed to fluster her. She felt comfortable, and though she tried to tell herself that she was relieved to have company in the big house, she knew now that it was much more than that. The week without Jeremy had served to show her how empty her life could truly be. For the first time Anne had to acknowledge that she wanted to have someone to share her accomplishments with. She had seen this week that independence fell short of what she wanted out of life.

"I moved the painting of Josiah and Dominique down to the library while you were gone. You may want it somewhere else, but I thought the library was the right place." Anne suddenly felt she was rambling, so she closed her mouth and turned away.

"That's fine. Just where I would have put it."

Anne ladled the hot chocolate into two mugs and sat down at the table with them. There didn't seem to be anything left to say. They faced each other across the table and sipped their drinks without speaking. The hot chocolate was sweet and warm, but the light brown liquid was tepid compared to the feeling that was radiating within her.

Anne warmed her cold fingers around her mug and looked across the shiny surface of the cocoa at Jeremy, who looked back at her. He had a relaxed, pleasant smile on his face, and as their eyes met and held, the steady gaze seemed to be speaking words that never formed on the lips or in the ear. Without an invitation Anne got up and went over to sit on his lap.

Jeremy accepted the gesture as if he had called her over. His arm wrapped itself around her small waist and she rested her head on his shoulder. Brushing a stray curl from her forehead, he planted a gentle kiss in its place.

"So, at last I learn the secret," he whispered in her ear. "All I had to do to win you over was leave you alone."

Anne didn't reply, but moved her head slightly to kiss the base of his neck. As she rested against his chest she could feel his voice more than hear it. Even in a whisper his voice had a deep, masculine vibration. She felt safe and secure in his arms, and wanted to stay there forever and forget all her responsibilities and obligations.

Jeremy lifted her chin, and once again they were eye to eye. His kiss was sweet and chocolaty, and Anne accepted it with a tiny giggle.

"What's funny?" he asked.

"Nothing. You just taste good."

"In that case I can only invite you to have seconds." He kissed her again, this time with greater feeling. Anne's lips relaxed and parted to accept his exploring tongue. She held on to his shoulders more tightly, savoring the wonderful, glowing sensation as his hand caressed the curve of her back. She opened a button on his shirt and slipped her hand inside to touch the springy hairs on his chest.

"*Hey*," he said suddenly, jerking back from her touch. "Your hands are *freezing*." Even after holding the hot mug, Anne's fingers were still cold.

"Cold hands, warm heart," Anne replied with an apologetic smile. Jeremy took her hands between his and warmed her fingers by rubbing them gently and kissing each fingertip in turn. Anne nuzzled the base of his neck and took little teasing bites of his warm, slightly salty skin.

Taking her face in his hands, Jeremy looked directly into her eyes. "You're playing with fire, princess. I hope you can deal with what you're starting."

"They're my matches and I suppose I can do what I want with them," Anne replied resolutely.

"Don't be flip, Anne. I don't want to love you tonight if you're going to throw a temper tantrum tomorrow morning."

"I hope we've had our last temper tantrum," Anne said sincerely. "I know what I said before, but I've had some time to think about it, Jeremy, and you were right. I was frightened. But I've seen something much more frightening now. I want to be with you, in every sense of the word. Everything was just happening too fast before. All this last week, when I've been alone, I just wanted you to come back."

"That's my girl," Jeremy said as he stood up, picking Anne up as he did. Her feet dangled in the air as he carried her down the hall. Mounting the stairs easily, as if she weighed no more than a rag doll, he brought her back to the room she hadn't entered since that first night.

The master bedroom was just as she remembered it—filled with the physical trappings of Jeremy's life. Anne sat on the edge of the bed with her knees drawn up as he laid a fire in the fireplace. He lit a thick, scented candle on the bureau, then turned off the lights. The only illumination in the room came from the flames, and Anne lay back to watch the flickering, wobbling shadows on the ceiling.

"Hello—remember me?" Jeremy said as he joined her on the bed.

"How could I forget?" Anne replied as she rolled over to put her arms round his neck. "You consume me even when you're not with me." His hands circled her waist and he pulled her over to straddle his hips. Anne slowly opened the buttons of his shirt as he lay passively, accepting her attentions.

She smoothed her fingers over the rough surface of his chest, caressing the swells of his muscles and letting her hands linger on his taut, flat abdomen. She was enjoying this role as the aggressor, and the feeling of excitement grew within her as she traced designs on Jeremy's firm flesh. Then, as he watched her with half-closed eyes, she slowly removed her own shirt, unbuttoning it and moving her shoulders to let the garment fall back gently.

"You've got a great future as an exotic dancer," Jeremy said with a smile as he reached up to cup the graceful swell of her breasts in his hands. Anne leaned forward, closer to his reach.

"I've been lying to you all the time about what I did before I came to Paradise," Anne said with a mischievous grin. "Actually, I was a stripper at the Empire Theater on Grand Circus Park."

"I caught a show there once," he replied with a twinkle in his eye. "Oh, just entertaining a business associate, you understand. Was that you? The girl who could twirl her tassels in opposite directions?"

Anne's face clouded with wonder. "Opposite directions? How?"

"She was very talented."

"But how could you do that?"

"I couldn't. Nothing to glue the tassels to."

Anne sat up straight and looked down at her chest. "I don't think I could twirl in one direction."

"You're getting distracted," Jeremy said as he rolled over to put Anne underneath him. She loved the sensation of his weight on top of her. His face hovered just a few scant inches above her own and his warm breath played over her skin. Her hands circled his back and caressed his shoulders.

Then Jeremy sat up, assuming the position that Anne had held just a few moments before. His fingers traced the swell of her breasts and he leaned over to take her delightfully sensitive nipples into his mouth and flick them playfully with his tongue.

"Oh," Anne sighed as her back arched in reponse to his ministrations. Her cheeks burned with the flush that had risen in them and her heart beat wildly.

Jeremy slid back a short distance so he could reach the placket of her slacks. He eased the zipper down and ran his fingers over the triangle of white panty he had exposed. Anne's hips rose to meet his touch, almost as if they had developed a mind of their own. He moved off her to slip the slacks down and discard them over the side of the bed, and a moment later his own jeans followed.

He lay down beside her again and the lengths of their bodies touched, awakening a deeper level of need within Anne. Jeremy's fingers hooked beneath the elastic of her panties and they gave way before him. Anne longed for him. Her legs parted as her hips rose to meet him.

But Jeremy did not enter her right away. His fingers slowly caressed the smooth skin of her thighs, gently exploring and finding the moist recess between her legs. Anne groaned with pleasure, losing all sense of time as he awakened her body to the joys of his lovemaking.

He rolled over and was on top of her and within her. The rhythm of their desire began slowly, gradually gaining in speed and intensity. Anne's breath was forced from her lungs in gasps as she climbed to the summit of her passion, ever higher, ever more desirous.

Then the world exploded in a burst of bright light. Anne's fingers grasped the muscles of Jeremy's back, as if to find an anchor in the real world. She heard a distant sound, then realized it was her own voice, answering Jeremy's cry of ecstasy. Their surroundings faded as they nestled in a world of their own, slowly descending until she found the bed below her and the comforting weight of Jeremy above her. She caressed his neck and shoulders, savoring the warm, slightly damp skin. The power and tension were gone from his muscles. He turned his head slightly and gently kissed her lips and eyelids before shifting his weight and pulling her into the crook of his arm. Anne turned to wrap herself around him and lay her head on his shoulder.

Relaxing against him, Anne listened to the regular sound of his breathing. Time seemed to stand still and she was content just to be touching Jeremy. There wasn't a problem in the world that could penetrate the capsule of contentment surrounding them.

After Anne's heart had settled into its normal rhythm and the flush had faded from her cheeks, she got up and crossed the room to the mirror over Jeremy's bureau. In the dim firelight her skin was smooth and pale, and she imagined that she looked almost childish with her small breasts and the smooth lines of her stomach and hips. Anne wondered that this small, youthful-looking body could have been in the grips of such violent feelings only a few moments before.

"Hey, where did you go?" Jeremy called from the bed. He was propped up on his elbows observing her as closely as she had been observing herself.

"I'm not far away," she replied with a smile. She turned back to the mirror and examined her breasts again. "That stripper," she said with a frown. "Was she bigger than me?"

"In what respect?"

"You know," Anne said cupping her hands under her small breasts.

"I don't remember," Jeremy said defensively.

"Yes, you do. Men remember that sort of thing."

"I refuse to answer on the grounds that it's going to make you self-conscious."

"I'm already self-conscious," Anne said, blushing.

"Come back here." Anne went back to the bed and knelt beside Jeremy. He reached up and ran his hand over the gentle swell of her bosom. "Just as I suspected. Perfectly adequate."

"But not spectacular?"

"I've always said that any more than a handful is a waste." Jeremy laughed as he pulled her across his lap. "Don't you dare start lookng into silicone implants or any such nonsense. I like you exactly as you are. You can't improve on some things."

Anne laughed. "I don't think I'd go that far."

"Good." His face descended to hers and engaged her in a warm kiss. As his hands moved down to explore her feminine curves she again experienced the wonderful feelings. Anne sighed and gave herself over to him, surrounded by a warmth and security she had never known before.

Chapter Eight

The remainder of autumn passed like the golden water over Tahquamenon Falls; Anne had never been so happy and at peace. As the weatherman had predicted, the sun shone and melted the snowman that she and Jeremy built, but something else they constructed that night endured.

Anne would always look back on those days of November and December as one of the most contented periods of her life. Work on the windows progressed steadily, and each afternoon brought the satisfaction of seeing more of the design assembled. In two weeks the first panel was complete, and Jeremy helped her install it in the library. His strength was necessary to lift the heavy panel of colored glass, but Anne contributed guidance and balance as they placed the window section in place and worked the putty around the edges to seal the frame.

Mrs. Harkness looked on throughout the process, wringing her hands and periodically warning them to "Look out" or "Be careful." Once, the panel swung out a little too far and it looked as if they were going to lose control of it. Mrs. Harkness gasped and clamped a nervous hand over her mouth in horror, but Jeremy shifted his weight slightly on the ladder and, with an extra measure of strength, brought the window back into alignment. Anne breathed a sigh of relief and

Mrs. Harkness collapsed, exhausted, into a chair. "I can't bear to watch," she said as she turned away.

Jeremy would have installed the moldings around the inside of the frame himself, but Anne insisted on helping. While Jeremy stood on the windowsill to nail the moldings in place, she handed up each piece of molding as he needed it and doled out the finishing nails a few at a time. Afterward, they both perched on the wide sill to stain and, later, to varnish the frame.

Anne found that she enjoyed working with Jeremy. He knew how to cooperate and had that most tactful of talents, the ability to give instructions without giving orders. He was in charge without pushing or shoving.

And much to Anne's delight, all the tension was gone from their personal relationship. Jeremy was affectionate, attentive, warm, and companionable. He kissed her often, and each touch awoke those womanly longings within her. She savored his company during the day and lovingly shared his bed at night.

On the day when Anne moved her belongings down from the room at the end of the hall, Jeremy made room in his closet by taking out all the clothes he didn't plan to wear in the near future and moving them upstairs. He brought her dresser down to put it next to his, and they replaced his coverlet with Anne's heirloom quilt. When they were finished, the room was no longer just Jeremy's; it was a place for both of them.

Anne worked on the stained-glass windows in her workshop through the ever shorter autumn days, and Jeremy worked upstairs remodeling the empty bedrooms. The odor of paint stripper and varnish competed with that of Mrs. Harkness's baking. Anne went upstairs to observe his progress whenever she took a break from her own work, and Jeremy came down periodically to look in on her. With each passing day, Anne more and more came to respect Jeremy's skill as a craftsman. He took pains to refinish the woodwork with a smooth, professional gloss and steamed the old wallpaper off the walls to replace it with neatly hung and perfectly matched new paper.

For several days one week, Anne set aside her work on the window to help Jeremy strip and refinish the oak floors in three of the bedrooms. They worked on their hands and knees spreading the stripper, then mopping the old varnish up with rags. When the floor was stripped to a dull blond sheen, they brushed new varnish over the old planks. The next day, when it had dried, they laid down a shine with paste wax and buffed it with a rented machine.

Jeremy hadn't actually come right out and asked her to help with the floors, and more than once Anne found herself amazed that she was actually doing something that had nothing to do with her window. He had simply commented that he was dreading the stripping job because of its sheer magnitude, and Anne suddenly heard a voice that sounded suspiciously like her own offering to help.

Through the messy, backbreaking job, they traded jokes and comfortable conversation. Anne learned that Jeremy's father had been a civil engineer, that his mother had wanted to be a writer but had never had anything published. It was his mother who had brought him to Paradise on all his summer vacations; Jeremy's father avoided his grandfather at all costs. She also learned that Jeremy's father was the youngest of four children and the only son. The three daughters had married and moved far from Michigan.

In the final analysis, Anne decided that she had offered to help because working with Jeremy was such a pleasure. Even if it was a difficult, tiring job, working beside him made it seem like fun. Just when the fumes of the stripping compound were getting to her, or the work of pushing a sticky rag back and forth over the tacky floor was becoming a bore, he would crack a silly joke or smile and wink at her, and Anne would wish that there were six floors to strip instead of three.

By mid-December the second main window panel went up and Anne couldn't help but feel that the work was going too fast. The greatest project of her life would soon be completed, and the two side windows wouldn't take long. Anne had no idea what would happen then. She wanted the process of building the great window to go on indefinitely.

Through those two peaceful, happy months, Anne would have been hard put to describe her relationship with Jeremy. It didn't fit into any easy pattern that she could talk about. They shared their meals at the kitchen table, admired each other's work, and helped each other when necessary. They spent many an evening in front of a crackling fire in the great library, sipping wine, talking quietly, sharing their thoughts. Jeremy held her with a warmth and protectiveness that soothed and excited her at the same time, and Anne discovered that there were as many expressions for love as there were nights. Sometimes Jeremy was the sophisticated seducer. At other times he was the gentle lover. She learned about the power and the tenderness that he was capable of, and she found that she could respond in as many ways as he could excite her.

In early December the snow came to stay, piling up in deep drifts around the windward side of the house. Every few days Jeremy would go out and shovel a path to the Blazer and the woodpile. As the snow outside got deeper, Anne came to appreciate the warmth and security of the Breck house more and

more. She knew that she would have spent a cold,
lonely winter down in her little shop. It was poorly
insulated and had always been drafty, so heating would
have been next to impossible—and the isolation . . . It
made her shiver just to think of it.

Three days before Christmas, Anne and Jeremy installed the third panel of the main window. Complete,
the design was breathtaking. The sunset behind the
hill glowed with an almost supernatural luminescence.
Anne's execution of the original design was not a copy
but an interpretation. Rather than faithfully reproduc-
ing the window in the old picture, she had added her
own touches. Amber glass in the downstairs windows
of the stained-glass house gave the impression that
someone was home with the lights on, and Anne had
added the old oak tree at the foot of the hill, now gone
in reality and unplanted in the day of the original
window but captured forever in the glass mosaic.

When the frames and moldings were in place, Jeremy and Anne stood back from the window and took
it in. Anne couldn't help but feel a surge of pride.
The afternoon sun shone through and brought the
great glass painting to blazing life. It cast random
patterns of red, green, and blue light over the library
floor and furniture, tinting the air with its brilliant
colors.

For a moment Anne was unaware of Jeremy's standing beside her as she looked at her finished work. She
felt torn. On the one hand, she was immensely proud
of her work. She had never done anything that compared with this window, and not too long ago she
might have been afraid to attempt such a massive
piece. Yet, here it was, lovingly created by her alone.

On the other hand, she felt regret that the window
was done. Working on it had been a heady experience,
giving a sense of purpose to her days that she had
never known before. She still had the two side win-

dows to build, but they would be lesser works. It wouldn't be the same as working on the main window.

"It's magnificent," Jeremy said in a hushed voice. Anne was startled by his voice, having almost forgotten he was there. "It's more beautiful than the original, more than I'd hoped for."

Anne blushed with pleasure. She had formed her own high opinion of the window, but to hear Jeremy praise it so was almost more satisfying than building the window itself. "Thank you," she replied quietly.

"Don't thank me, thank you," Jeremy said. "It's wonderful."

"Thank you for giving me the opportunity to do it. I might have made my little sun catchers for years without getting the opportunity to do a job like this. Your faith in my ability is as responsible for that window as I am."

"I had a feeling about you, the moment I saw you, Anne Keene. I said to myself, this lady doesn't belong in this little shack of a shop, and you proved me right. Earning an extra thousand, I might add."

Anne was jarred by the mention of money. As she had worked on the window she hadn't thought about Jeremy's bonus. She had finished the window by Christmas almost in spite of herself, and now the mention of the bonus seemed out of place, almost disrespectful. It hurt her to think that Jeremy thought she had been rushing the job to earn the extra money.

"You don't have to pay me a bonus," she said, trying to disguise the hurt in her voice. "After all, I've been living here for two months without paying room and board. Besides, you've paid me enough for the windows already. I wouldn't feel right taking any more money from you."

Jeremy looked puzzled by her refusal. "Room and board? That hardly seems appropriate under the circumstances. I wouldn't turn the bonus down if I were you, Anne,—it's good money."

"I'm sure it is," she said, now letting some of her feelings show. "But I'm sure you love it much more than I would, so why not let it stay where it's appreciated?"

Jeremy looked even more mystified. "I'm sorry. I didn't mean any insult. It's what we agreed on."

"It's what *you* agreed on," Anne said through pursed lips. "I was just along for the ride." She walked away from Jeremy toward the window. When she got close to it, she pretended to examine the solder joints near the bottom of the center section. When she stopped to think about her own behavior, she was almost as mystified as Jeremy. She was near tears and didn't know why. Offering to pay her the money he had promised certainly wasn't an insult or slight to her work, so why had it hurt so badly?

Jeremy came to the window to stand beside her, his face full of concern. "What's the matter?" he asked gently.

"I don't know. I'm sorry, I didn't mean to say that. I guess I just don't feel like talking about money right now."

"I think you're just feeling let down because the biggest part of the job is done. It can be like that when you work very hard on a special project for a long time. While you're doing it you can't wait to get it done and see how it's going to work out. Then you finish it, and you realize you've got to let it go. I suppose it's something like raising a child and then having to watch him grow up and leave home. While you're working on it it's all yours. Now that it's done, it belongs to the world."

Anne managed a wan smile. "It doesn't belong to the world, Jeremy, it belongs to you."

"It only partially belongs to me," Jeremy said with

a smile. "It also belongs to Josiah and Dominique." He gestured at the painting that now hung over the fireplace with a perfect view of the window. "And to Florence and Morton, and to all the people who will come here as guests. They'll all take a piece of it away with them in their memories. But most of all, it will always belong to you. You put a lot of yourself into it and nobody will ever be able to separate you from it."

Anne looked up into Jeremy's face. A wedge of emerald-green light spilled across the bridge of his nose and the rosy pink of the glass sunset colored his forehead. He looked as if he were wearing clown makeup, but the sincerity of his expression kept Anne from laughing. His face descended to hers and their lips met in a kiss. Anne sighed, relaxing against the warm, firm muscles of Jeremy's chest as the tension flowed out of her. She felt and heard Jeremy's deep chuckle.

"What's so funny?"

"I can't believe I just kissed a woman with green hair."

"I'd rather have green hair than a green nose."

Christmas Eve, Jeremy went into the woods with an ax and came back with a small pine tree, setting it up in the library near the newly completed window. He brought a box of ornaments down from upstairs, and as he built a fire in the fireplace Anne untangled the old strings of lights and tested them for burned-out bulbs. Mrs. Harkness had spent the afternoon stringing popcorn, and now the room was full of golden firelight and scented with pine needles and popcorn. Anne hadn't felt this excited about a Christmas since she was a little girl.

Feeling festive, she'd dressed in a red taffeta blouse with ruffles down the front and a gray wool skirt. She circled her waist with a gold chain-link belt and put on a pair of high-heeled, open-toed sandals to match. Gold barrettes and crystal teardrop earrings completed her outfit. Even if she and Jeremy would be spending the evening by themselves, Anne felt that dressing up was part of the holiday.

She had gone into town with Mrs. Harkness the previous afternoon and spent hours searching through the few stores that stayed open through the winter for the perfect gift for Jeremy. Just anything wouldn't do; it had to be something special. After rejecting every tie clasp, cuff link, key chain, and bottle of after-shave in Paradise, Anne found a small antiques store near the public library. She was even about to give up on that when she found it. A miner's hat with a built-in lantern was buried in a corner behind a stack of old tools. Closer inspection revealed the words BRECK COPPER MINE stamped inside. Anne was delighted, knowing it was perfect. She had the shop-keeper wrap the old hard hat in tissue paper and smuggled it into the house when she got back.

Anne had wrapped it in colorful Christmas paper, and now she was dying for Jeremy to see it. When the tree was decorated and he had finished by putting the angel on top, Anne with all the enthusiasm of a small child, ran upstairs and brought down her package. To her surprise, and pleasure, Jeremy had brought out a smaller package in her absence. The hat made a rather lumpy bundle, since Anne hadn't been able to find a box to put it in, but she had tied a large ribbon on it just the same. She put the odd-shaped package under the tree and stopped to look at the tiny square box Jeremy had placed there.

It was wrapped in green tissue paper without any ribbon. A small card on top said "To Anne" in Jeremy's precise handwriting. Anne wondered when he had gone out to buy it but decided he must have slipped out while she was shopping with Mrs. Harkness. Because of its small size, Anne felt sure the gift was a piece of jewelry.

"For me?" Anne asked with a delighted smile.

"No, it's for Anne Smith. She should be here any minute."

"Don't tease. Can I open it now?"

"No, you have to wait until I say so."

"When will that be?"

"Later," Jeremy said with exaggerated casualness.

"Well, if you can wait, so can I," Anne countered. They brought out a plate of Mrs. Harkness's fruitcake, and Jeremy poured spiced punch into two crystal goblets. The glasses rang delicately as Anne and Jeremy clicked them together in a toast.

"To the most beautiful woman in Paradise," Jeremy said with a smile.

Anne blushed and cast her eyes down.

"Ah, that lovely blush." He chuckled. "Women throughout the world smear their cheeks with rouge trying to achieve what you do without even trying."

"Stop it," Anne said. "You've got me going and if you don't stop I'll be glowing like a traffic light."

"But I love it. I'll stop at your corner anytime." Jeremy took the goblet out of Anne's hand and set it aside. "It's time now."

"That certainly wasn't very long."

"To tell the truth, I just can't wait any longer to see what that strangely shaped thing under the tree is."

Anne smiled in anticipation. "All right. Just to prove that I'm stronger than you, you go first."

Jeremy carefully unwrapped Anne's gift. When it was open and the paper lay discarded on the floor, Anne could see that she had found the right present.

"I'm amazed," he said. "Where did you find this? The mine closed down almost eighty years ago. I didn't think there was anything left around here.

Antiques dealers from the East cleaned out Paradise years ago."

"It was in that little antiques store near the library. I almost didn't find it. But when I saw it, it just cried out, 'I'm for Jeremy.' "

"Hmm, it's surprisingly reticent now."

"All right. It's my turn." Jeremy handed her the little package. Anne's fingers trembled as she opened the paper to find the tiny velvet-covered box inside, and she felt strangely clumsy as she rushed to open it. When the lid was finally up, Anne was confused. A jeweled pendant with a fine, braided silver chain lay nestled in the satin lining.

The necklace was an artistic piece of jewelry. Spidery lines of filigree wound around the edges, and a large ruby surrounded by smaller diamonds graced the center. Anne had no doubt that the stones were real—Jeremy Breck didn't waste his time with imitations. As she examined the fine workmanship of the necklace she knew that it was an antique. Jeremy hadn't gone out to find her a gift; this necklace had to be a family heirloom.

"It's beautiful," Anne whispered.

"It's only as beautiful as the lady who wears it," Jeremy replied. He took the necklace and stepped behind her to place it around her neck. Anne looked down and the ruby flashed against the red material of her blouse. She turned to look up into Jeremy's eyes.

"I don't know what to say."

He chuckled. "Try 'Thank you.' "

"I don't know how to begin thanking you," Anne said sincerely. "I never would have made it through this winter without your help, Jeremy. If I've seemed ungrateful for all you've done for me, it was just my thoughtlessness. The chance to do this window, letting me live here—even after I was so nasty about it—and now this beautiful gift. You've changed my life. I'd be nothing but miserable, lonely, and broke today if you hadn't come into my shop that night."

Jeremy's brow wrinkled ever so slightly at her words, as if he were displeased at what she was saying. But the cloud passed from his face as quickly as it had come, and Anne couldn't be sure of what she had seen. His eyes were firmly upon her, boring into her as if looking for something. If only she knew what. She wanted so badly to say exactly the right thing—to give him whatever it was that he wanted.

He turned away from her and she felt a keen sense of disappointment. She had failed somehow. She had said or done the wrong thing, and the pendant seemed to weigh heavily around her neck. Anne took it in her hand, looking into the ruby as if the answer were hidden there. Why this particular present? Was the gift of a family heirloom asking for a commitment, or was it just something convenient? Something that just happened to be around. A nice gesture but nothing more.

"I've never had a piece of jewelry as nice as this," she said after a long silence. "Whose was it?"

"Dominique's. I thought you might like to have something of hers."

"Yes, that makes it even more special." Anne stepped closer to Jeremy and looked up into his face, hoping to see a sign that he meant something more. The eyes that looked down at her were warm and tender with the twinkle of Christmas lights reflected in their depths. She felt the hard shape of the pendant press against her breast as he pulled her close, his lips meeting hers in a kiss of undeniable passion.

"You *are* the most beautiful woman in Paradise, Anne," he whispered in her ear.

Anne stepped away from Jeremy and picked up her goblet of punch. "To the most wonderful Christmas I can ever remember," she said with a warm smile.

Jeremy seated himself on the couch next to the fire and beckoned to Anne to join him. Anne sat down, watching the dancing flames for a few moments as Jeremy draped his arm around her shoulders.

"We didn't hang any stockings," she said suddenly.

Jeremy laughed. "You really are a traditionalist. I didn't think of it."

"Oh, that's all right. I don't need any stocking stuffers. I've got everything I want right here."

"Me too." He pulled her closer and began to nibble on the sensitive lobe of her ear.

"Do you suppose that Josiah and Dominique sat here, just as we are now, on Christmas Eve a hundred years ago?" she asked.

"Probably not."

"Why not?"

"Josiah always used to throw a huge Christmas Party for all his employees on Christmas Eve. They'd have punch and Christmas cookies and cakes and little gifts for the children down at the Methodist Church. It went on until midnight, when they would end the party with a candlelight church service. Of course in those days they weren't going for atmosphere when they held a candlelight service."

"But then they came back here by themselves," Anne prompted.

"Yes, but they probably just fell into bed exhausted. Dominique would have done all the cooking for the party and Josiah would have made all the arrangements. And he took all the families home who lived any distance from the church if they didn't have their own carriage. He'd hook up a hay wagon behind his team of Percheron horses, and they would have a hay ride to pick everybody up and drop them off at their homes."

Anne looked up at the portrait hanging over the

mantel. "He really cared about the people who worked for him."

"I think so. If you listen to the stories about Josiah, especially about his later life, you'll hear that he was a skinflint who never let go of a penny until he had squeezed every drop of blood out of it. Yet if you look at his personal accounts, you'll see that he paid the medical bills for his employees who were laid up and couldn't work. He paid the bills for their families, too. That was long before group health insurance and union benefits."

Anne chuckled. "It was long before three-hundred-dollar-a-day hospital rooms, too."

"True. But Josiah really looked upon the welfare of his people as his responsibility. As long as his workers were working for his benefit, he looked after them." Jeremy took Anne's chin between his thumb and forefinger and turned her head gently so that she was facing him. "But enough about the old folks," he said with a smile. "If there are ghosts, they aren't home. They're in town giving their annual party at the Methodist Church for the ghosts of the workers. We're really alone tonight."

"I've never minded having them around," Anne replied. "As family ghosts go, they seem to be very well behaved."

Jeremy didn't answer. His arms closed tightly around her, drawing her into an ardent embrace. Later, when Anne lay stretched out on the couch, with only the ruby pendant glistening in the firelight against her pale breasts, she wondered how it was possible to feel as satisfied as she felt at the moment. The lights from the Christmas tree threw twinkling colored patterns on the ceiling, the heat from the fireplace warmed her bare skin, and Jeremy's head rested against her hip as he sat on the floor next to her sipping his punch. Anne's hand dangled off the edge of the couch to touch his bare shoulder. She felt as if the perfection surrounding her was shadowy and insubstantial. She must lie perfectly still; if she moved, the dream she was living would end and she would wake in a different place, a different time, and find that she had imagined everything. Surely no one was this content this side of Heaven.

Chapter Nine

Jeremy leaned toward the entry-hall mirror, trimming the rough edges of his mustache with a small pair of scissors. Anne was coming downstairs when she spotted him in this odd attitude. Looking very handsome in his gray flannel three-piece suit, he was totally immersed in the job of making his already attractive mustache perfect.

"Where are you going?" Anne asked as she reached the bottom of the stairs.

"Nowhere. What makes you think I'm going anyplace?"

"You're hardly dressed for hanging wallpaper."

"Oh," he said, looking down at his suit. "We're having company today. Very important company."

Anne considered her navy-blue gabardine slacks and plaid cotton blouse, wondering if she ought to change.

"Who's coming? I positively refuse to dress up unless I know whom it's for."

Jeremy finished with the scissors and examined his jacket carefully for lint. "Michael Barnes," he said cryptically.

"*Oh*," Anne exclaimed, laughing. "Michael Barnes. Not *the* Michael Barnes? All right, I'll bite. Who's Michael Barnes?"

"Only the most important person in the world—at least as far as the Paradise Inn is concerned. He's the reason I wanted the main window done so early. He's a writer for *American Vacation* magazine and will be doing a feature on the Paradise Inn. A spread in *AV* can make or break a new place like this."

Anne nodded in agreement. "But tell me, Jeremy, why are you dressing?"

"For success, my dear. *Success.*"

Anne chuckled. "That outfit may say success in Chicago, but it seems a little out of place for a northern Michigan innkeeper. You look as if you're on your way to foreclose on a mortgage."

Jeremy looked down at his suit again. "You think it's too much?"

Anne nodded. "Why don't you go a bit more casual? Maybe your gray turtleneck and a navy-blue sports jacket."

"I'll bow to your artistic sense of style," Jeremy replied, "but he's supposed to be here any minute. Would you mind greeting him while I change?"

"My pleasure," Anne said with a smile.

After Jeremy went upstairs, Anne went to the front window and looked out over the snow-covered lawn. Three weeks had passed since Christmas, and the weather was milder than usual for the Upper Peninsula. Although snow continued to cover the ground, they had yet to be snowed in. Getting into town was no problem.

The first of the two side windows in the library was complete and installed, and the second window was well under way. Before long, the job that had brought her to Jeremy's house would be finished. Anne wondered what would happen then.

Before Jeremy finished changing, a car pulled up the drive and a short man in a rumpled car coat and carrying a camera bag got out. Anne opened the door and welcomed him.

"You must be Michael Barnes," she said in the

entry hall, extending her hand. Michael Barnes accepted her handshake with a limp and sweaty hand.

"And I suppose you're Mrs. Breck?"

"Uh, no. Anne Keene."

The writer didn't seem terribly embarrassed by his gaffe, but Anne tried to smooth things over just the same.

"Jeremy will be down in a moment," Anne said with a warm smile. "He's very pleased that your magazine is going to do a piece about the Paradise Inn."

Michael Barnes made a slightly unpleasant face and Anne gave him a questioning look.

"Oh, I just love trekking to the wilderness to do a puff piece on a hotel that isn't even open yet," he said sourly. "But a sacred cow is a sacred cow, if you take my meaning."

Anne didn't take his meaning, but she knew for sure that she didn't like this man. She recognized the importance of a favorable article in the magazine, however, so she disguised her feelings.

"You may be pleasantly surprised," Anne said with a carefully composed smile. "There's some very interesting history connected with this house."

"Just like every other house in the United States with more than two bedrooms," he said with a snort. "However, the newsworthy aspect of this abode is the fact that it is owned by the ex-president and ex-husband of the chairman of the board of the bank that holds most of the loans owed by American Vacation Publishing."

"Then you have a wonderful angle for your story. Banker opts for the simple life and all that," Anne said with a smile set in cement.

"Save it for *Mother Earth*," the writer said with a sneer.

"Well, in any case, let me take your coat," Anne said through clenched teeth. She helped him out of the grubby garment and noticed a missing button and several rips in the lining as she hung it on the coat tree. As she turned back to him she saw that his clothes were no better. His shirt had sweat stains under the arms, and his shirt and pants were wrinkled. His knit tie showed several grease spots. He was a slightly chubby, soft-looking man with thin, stringy hair and unpleasantly small features lost in a wide face.

"I don't know why it's always someone else who gets to do the Hawaiian Paradise piece. Why do I always get stuck with the Arctic Circle?" Anne tried to imagine this ugly little man interviewing tanned beauties on a Hawaiian beach, but failed.

"It's probably because you're the kind of writer who can make anything sound good," Anne said, lying shamefully.

"That's the reward I get for being good," the writer sighed.

Anne wondered what was taking Jeremy so long. If he didn't get down here quickly, she was going to clobber this jerk, publicity or no publicity.

"So, if you're not Mrs. Breck, you must be the housekeeper?"

"No," Anne replied, barely concealing her contempt. "I'm building stained-glass windows for the library."

Just when Anne's patience was stretched to the breaking point, Jeremy appeared at the top of the stairs, wearing the outfit she had suggested.

"Mr. Barnes," he said heartily. "Welcome to the Paradise Inn." He came down the stairs and pumped the writer's hand enthusiastically. Michael Barnes smiled perfunctorily.

"Well, let's get on with this," he said in a bored voice. "I want to catch the noon flight out of this hole."

Anne thought she saw a shadow of anger pass across Jeremy's eyes, but his smile stayed in place.

"In that case let's start with the grand tour," he said, leading the writer down the hall. Anne went to her workshop, content to be away from Michael Barnes. The man had all the endearing qualities of a garden slug.

She worked halfheartedly for a while, not really interested in doing anything, just wanting to stay away from the annoying Mr. Barnes. But far sooner than she would have hoped, Jeremy's tour found its way to her hiding place.

"And this is where Anne builds the windows," Jeremy said as he brought the little man into her inner sanctum. Michael Barnes looked bored, but he had his camera out and he snapped several pictures of her workshop.

"Now I'd like a picture of the two of you together," the writer said. "Why don't you go over there and point something out to her on that window she's working on?" Jeremy complied and Anne smoothed her hair before assuming an attitude of work.

"Okay, now, how about something a little more friendly? Go behind her and look over her shoulder." He took another picture. "All right, that should do it. Let's get the interview over with."

"We'll be more comfortable in the library," Jeremy said. "I'll have Mrs. Harkness bring us some coffee and a snack. You go on back and I'll be there in a moment." Michael Barnes left and as soon as his back was turned, Jeremy made a face. "He's impossible," Jeremy whispered to Anne. "I'm going to kill him before we're finished."

"I know exactly what you mean," Anne whispered back. "If you decide to get violent, let me know—I want to help."

"You can help right now by coming down to the library. He may be a little safer if there's a witness in the room."

Anne frowned.

"Please? Don't leave me alone with him."

She couldn't help but laugh. "All right, but you owe me one."

Anne went to the library while Jeremy went to give instructions to Mrs. Harkness. As she walked into the room she interrupted the writer poking around in a bookcase, possibly testing for secret panels.

"If you're looking for the closet with the skeletons, I don't think you'll find it," Anne said as pleasantly as she could. "We're very open and aboveboard here."

The writer started when she spoke, but showed no shame at having been caught.

"Nice woodwork," he said, gesturing at the bookcase.

"Yes, it is. Solid oak."

"So, Annie, if I can call you that, what exactly is your relationship to Mr. Back-to-the-Simple-Life?"

None of your business was the answer that popped into her head, but Anne discarded that in favor of a more tactful route. "Friendly, *Mr.* Barnes, quite friendly." Anne hoped that her emphasis on the word "Mister" conveyed the message that she didn't want him to use her first name, let alone call her Annie.

"Is that so, Annie? Does that mean your dance card has some empty space on it? If so, I could stretch my expense account to stay in Upper Arctic Hicksville for a couple of days."

Anne was flabbergasted. The little creep was actually presumptuous enough to come on to her! In Anne's entire vocabulary there didn't seem to be a comeback acidic enough to fit the situation. She remembered, just in time, that she had to be nice to him. She took a deep breath. "Sorry," she said carefully. "I seem to be pretty solidly booked for the next week or so." Anne had the sudden feeling that someone was watching her and glanced over her shoulder. Jeremy had come into the room just in time to catch this last exchange.

There was a strong look of displeasure on his face, but he composed himself before Michael Barnes bothered to notice.

"Well, has Anne been telling you about her window?" Jeremy said as he seated himself next to her on the couch.

"It's not half bad," the writer replied. "I understand that this is your first major window. Have you been working in glass for long?"

Much to Anne's surprise, once his mind was turned to the matter at hand, Michael Barnes turned out to be a reasonably professional and facile interviewer. His questions were perceptive and he listened carefully to the answers, making a lot of notes. If his behavior improved, however, his personal habits didn't. When Mrs. Harkness brought in a pot of coffee and a freshly baked apple pie, he managed to slosh coffee on the tabletop and dribble pie crumbs down the front of his shirt. He ate his slice of pie greedily and Anne found that watching him killed her appetite.

In the course of the interview, Jeremy explained his reasons for having given up the executive's life, his plans for the inn, the history of the house and a little about the town of Paradise. In response to the writer's questions, Anne talked about her methods for working in stained glass, her reasons for giving up her accounting job, and her decision to come to Paradise.

When asked about her plans for the future, Anne fumbled. The question filled her with panic. "I really haven't given that much thought," she said uncertainly. "After I finish this job, I suppose I'll find something else to do. I guess I'll be reopening my shop down on the highway come spring." She wished she could have sounded more positive, but she just didn't know. She hadn't dared think about what would happen when the windows were finished. Jeremy wasn't going to kick her out as soon as her work was done, but spring

would come, and the question of reopening her shop
was bound to come up. Anne had simply chosen not to
think about that.

Jeremy stepped in to rescue her. "Of course, we're
going to decorate with Anne's stained-glass sun catchers here in the inn, and we'll have an arrangement to
sell them on consignment."

Anne blushed as Jeremy spoke. She was glad that
he had said something, if only to take Michael Barnes's
attention away from her, but she was a little surprised to find that Jeremy had plans beyond the immediate future and that he had never discussed them
with her. Yet his answer still didn't settle anything;
he'd said nothing about her shop.

Michael Barnes nodded and scribbled a few more
notes. "What about the rest of these windows?" he
said, gesturing around the room.

"Anne is doing another window for the frame to the
right of the big window," Jeremy explained, "but the
rest of them will stay clear. I think any more stained
glass in here would be overpowering." Jeremy stood
up and went over to the fireplace. "These are the
house's original owners," he said, waving at the painting over the mantel. "The painting was done by Thomas
Eakins, you know."

"Really?" Michael Barnes got up and went to examine the painting closely. "So this is the old man and
his squaw. Just a minute, I want to get another picture."
He went back and got his camera, snapping a picture
of Jeremy as he stood under the painting.

Anne let the two men recede from her mind as they
walked to the fireplace. She could think only about
Jeremy's statement about selling her sun catchers on
consignment. It was an acknowledgment on his part
that her job here was almost done and she would soon
be continuing her own work, but that wasn't a real
answer. She knew she could continue to build win-

dows and sun catchers even if she remained at the Paradise Inn with Jeremy. That might even be a convenient arrangement. She could turn her workshop into a salesroom and sell to the guests, as well as to tourists who just passed through.

But her shop was *her* shop; she had worked hard to establish it, and the idea of abandoning it made a lump rise in Anne's throat.

Still, she didn't want to leave the house. She could tell herself that it was because this was a much more comfortable place to live than her little shop, but that was a lie and she knew it.

She couldn't deny the real reason. She was in love with Jeremy Breck and she didn't want to be away from him. Not even for a short time, let alone for the rest of her life.

"Just one more picture," Michael Barnes was saying. Anne snapped to attention and found that Jeremy and the writer had come back from the fireplace and were standing just behind where she was sitting. "You and Annie sitting on the windowsill," he continued. He positioned them facing each other on the sill, knees drawn up with their toes touching. "That's great. With the light coming through it will make a good silhouette shot." Michael Barnes took the picture, then started to put his camera away. "I think that ought to do it," he said. "If I step on it, I can still make my plane."

"Well, I certainly appreciate your coming," Jeremy said with a smile. "And once we're open, you're welcome to come back anytime."

"Sure," the writer said unenthusiastically.

"Let me get your coat," Anne said.

In the hall, out of Jeremy's earshot, he leaned over and whispered, *sotto voce,* "Just say the word, babe, and I could miss that plane." Anne thought she was going to choke.

"You'd better hurry. I'd hate to think of your having to wait for another flight," she said sweetly.

As soon as the front door was shut and Michael Barnes was on his way, Jeremy came out of the library and groaned. "I'm going to call my friend Marshall Morrison, publisher of *AV*, and ask him which rock he found that thing under."

"No, don't." Anne laughed, leaning against the door as if to prevent Michael Barnes from reentering. "He may be a slimy little creature, but I think he knows his business and he'll write a good article. You'll just stir up trouble if you call his boss to complain."

"You're probably right. But I've never had to tolerate anyone so rude. Am I mistaken, or did I walk in as he was making a pass at you?"

"You're not mistaken." Anne giggled helplessly. "I wonder if he tries that on every woman he meets. I don't know about anyone else, but I wouldn't go to Heaven with that man if Gabriel was blowing his horn."

"It's not funny," Jeremy said with a frown. But then he rolled his eyes and laughed ruefully. "I invited him to come back anytime. But I swear that if he ever does show up, I'm going to close the door and nail it shut."

"Well, he's gone, and that's the best thing I can think of to say about Michael Barnes."

"By the way, thank you. You were a great help."

"My pleasure. Almost."

"Well, I'm going to change back into my work clothes," Jeremy said as he started up the stairs.

Chapter Ten

Anne regretted installing the final window, but not as much as she would have if that had meant her moving out of Jeremy's house. Living here without the excuse of her work seemed strange, but Anne accepted the strangeness with a blind eye because staying kept her close to Jeremy and being close to Jeremy seemed the most important thing she could think of. Continuing to defer her decision about the future of her shop, she let each day provide its own challenges, triumphs, and pleasures.

Anne often thought about that first night she and Jeremy had spent together, and her original protest that she couldn't work on Jeremy's windows and sleep with him at the same time. What a strange thought that seemed now, Anne mused. She could only look upon that earlier attitude as foolishness now. What did her undeniable attraction to Jeremy have to do with her work? Nothing, absolutely nothing.

January turned to February, February turned to March, and a deadline loomed ahead of Anne. Jeremy had set April 15 as the date when the Paradise Inn would open for business. That would mark the official beginning of the tourist season, and before that day she had to decide whether there would still be a Keene's Kraft Kabin. One day she would think that she could continue to live at the Paradise Inn and keep her shop open during the day, but the next day that seemed an absurd idea. After creating the window, how could she bear to spend her days sitting in that little shack by the highway, waiting for a mere trickle of customers?

Through agreements with several travel agents, the Paradise Inn was becoming known, even if it wasn't nationally prominent yet. Reservations were starting to come in and Anne spent part of each day keeping records of future guests and answering letters of inquiry from potential guests. She set up a bookkeeping system to handle the room deposits, and Jeremy complimented her on her work. She was aware that these minor tasks were something that Jeremy could have handled easily with his business experience, but working at something she was well trained at gave her a feeling of usefulness. She found the bookkeeping far more interesting than her old job, possibly because Jeremy let her work out her own methods without any of the interference she'd always encountered from Mr. Masters.

When she wasn't working on the books, Anne helped Jeremy renovate the remaining upstairs rooms. Painting, wallpapering, and varnishing suited her artistic talents and she found the work pleasant and satisfying.

The final task in the renovation was choosing the new bedding, curtains, and linen, and in this job Jeremy deferred entirely to Anne, saying that he was sure she would do it better because she was so artistic. Anne spent several wonderful days choosing bedspreads, curtains, sheets, and towels in different pastel floral motifs for each room. Her favorite was the one at the end of the hall that had once been hers. She chose white eyelet priscilla curtains and an ivory linen bedspread with delicately embroidered flowers. Sheets and pillowcases with eyelet lace edging and ivory towels completed the decor, and the effect was light and airy, with a definitely romantic touch. When

Jeremy saw her selections for the room, he approved heartily, dubbing the room the Honeymoon Suite. Anne argued that a suite had to have more than one room, but Jeremy only laughed and called her a nitpicker.

Jeremy set up the reception desk in the first room off the entry hall. Rather than building a traditional counter and pigeonhole arrangement, he set up a writing stand that held the guest register, a quill pen, and a cut-glass inkwell. The serious record keeping for the inn was done at an antique mahogany desk in the corner. He put a key rack on the wall to hold the six room keys, then installed a small wooden box on each room door to hold messages that came for the guests.

In early March there was a partial thaw, and the long, clear icicles began their slow journey down from the eaves of the Paradise Inn. The crystal stalactites grew steadily longer outside the windows and under the edge of the front porch roof as the drops of water beat a muffled tattoo on the melting snow. Anne sat at the mahogany desk and tried to keep her mind on updating the reservations, but she found herself watching the water drip from the end of a particularly long icicle as she daydreamed. Reservations were coming in at a steady rate and something about the idea of guests coming to the Paradise Inn made her feel uneasy. She had been booking reservations for weeks now, but every time she recorded the arrival date of a future guest, Anne felt slightly resentful; this had become her home, and these people didn't have any right coming here. They were going to change everything. She allowed these uncomfortable thoughts, then chided herself for being childish. The purpose of the Paradise Inn was to have guests.

Anne wondered what would happen on the day the first guests arrived with their luggage and their vacation plans and their lives that had nothing to do with Jeremy and herself.

She watched the steady drip of water off the end of the icicle and wondered what Jeremy would say if she were to announce that she was moving back to her shop as soon as the tourist season began. He'd be furious, she thought. Or would he? She didn't really want to move back to her shop . . .

She was brought back from her reverie by the sound of the front door opening and closing. Jeremy, having gone to the mailbox, had returned.

"Anne," he called. "Look what *I've* got." His voice was full of enthusiasm.

Anne came out into the hall to find him holding a magazine in a brown paper wrapper. She took it from him while he took off his coat, and closer inspection showed it to be the March issue of *American Vacation* magazine. Anne started to remove the wrapper but Jeremy snatched it back from her.

He laughed. "Oh, no, you don't. *I* get to look first."

Anne pretended to grapple for the magazine like an impatient child, laughing all the time. "Aw, come on. Let *me* see it."

"When I'm done." Jeremy was laughing and holding the magazine over his head so that Anne couldn't reach it. He led the way to the library, holding the magazine like a beacon all the way.

As he sat down on a couch he motioned to Anne to sit beside him. "Sit down and behave and maybe I'll let you look," he teased. Anne sat down primly, folding her hands in her lap and waiting a moment before making a dive for the magazine. Jeremy kept her back easily and held the prize out at arm's length. Finally Jeremy composed himself and slipped the wrapper off the magazine.

His eyes opened wide when he saw the cover; the two of them were silhouetted against the brilliant colors of the stained-glass window.

"With all of Michael Barnes's obvious faults, he is one fantastic photographer," he said appreciatively.

"The magazine had to have some reason to keep him around," Anne replied. "It certainly wasn't for his good looks or sparkling personality."

"The front cover—this is better than I'd hoped for. You know what this means? This summer we'll be turning the guests away."

"Hurry up and look inside," Anne prompted.

"All in good time." Jeremy held out the magazine and looked at the cover from the end of his arm. After another look he opened it to the contents page and found the article page number. The piece was a beautiful photo spread showing different aspects of the house, leading off with the photo of Anne working as Jeremy looked over her shoulder.

Something in the back of Anne's mind started to bother her. Something was wrong, but she couldn't quite tie it down. Why was she so prominent in the article? It should be about Jeremy and the inn, but as they flipped through the pages quickly, Anne found that all three of the pictures she had been in were used. In the third picture, the one in which Jeremy had stood across the workbench from her, Jeremy had been cropped out and she alone sat working at her glass. Anne frowned.

"Why did they use so many pictures of me?" she asked uncomfortably.

"Because pretty women sell magazines." Jeremy laughed and leaned over to kiss her on the cheek.

"But the article is supposed to be about *you*."

"I haven't been ignored," Jeremy replied. He flipped back to the beginning of the article and started to read in a dramatic intonation:

A presence has returned to the sleepy little resort town of Paradise, Michigan. A force long absent has returned to settle in its own place. Things are going to change in this town, which has all but lain dormant for the better part of this century. You can feel it in the air. And if any newcomers—people whose families have been here less than a century—wonder what is going on, the answer is simple: a Breck is in Paradise and all's right with the world.

Anne was incredulous. "Don't you think that's a bit much?" she asked.

"No one could say that Mr. Barnes's writing style is bland," Jeremy chuckled.

" 'Purple' is the word I think you're looking for. He makes it sound as if you were going to redevelop the whole town."

"Well, he's not completely wrong. The business and publicity that the inn will bring to Paradise is going to do everybody some good. This has become a forgotten backwater. There's some tourism, but not so much as the area could support. This article and word-of-mouth from the people who visit the inn are going to put Paradise back on the map."

Anne chuckled. "I think you're starting to believe your own press releases."

"Well, let's see what else he has to say." Anne and Jeremy read silently through the article together. She had to admit that it was compellingly written; if she hadn't been here already, she would have started making plans to relocate. Michael Barnes wrote about the unusual architecture and equated it with the strong will of the builder. He recounted the history of the Breck family, as Jeremy had told it, and tied the story to the history of the area. Apparently, he had done some library research before coming to the house, and Anne's respect for his writing talent grew as she read.

But that nagging, something's-not-right feeling grew

as Anne read on. When she got to the section of the article about the library windows, the bottom fell out.

> The current master of the house has taken measures to return it to its former glories, and nowhere is that more evident than in the library. Josiah Breck had the great stained-glass library windows built in Europe. Time and vandalism have destroyed those great works of glass art, but Jeremy Breck has replaced the windows, with the help of his artist-mistress, Anne Keene.

Anne's eyes stuck on the word "mistress," refusing to read any farther. She pointed to the word and said angrily, "That little *twerp*."

"What?" Jeremy looked up from the page.

"He referred to me as your *mistress*."

"Don't get so upset. Just read on. He's very complimentary about you."

Anne forced herself to continue. Indeed, Michael Barnes was very complimentary about her work. In fact, he bordered on the embarrassing with his profuse praise, but Anne wasn't mollified.

"Where did he get that idea?" she asked. "He was even coming on to me. Why would he write this way about me?"

"Has it occurred to you that when he made his pass he was really trying to see where your loyalties lay?"

"It wasn't much of a test. I wouldn't have gone out with him if I were living alone at the North Pole."

"I don't think he has the clear picture of his lack of charm that we do. People tend to be blind to their own faults."

"Be that as it may, he's got nerve. Turn the page. I want to see how this article ends."

"I already looked. It gets pretty boring at the end," Jeremy said in a strange voice. Jeremy had peeked at the next page while Anne was still reading about the window.

"Let me see."

"You don't want to see it. You'll be happier if you don't."

"Give me the magazine, Jeremy, I *mean* it."

Jeremy sighed and handed it over. "Believe me, I didn't tell him to write what's on the last page. I'm afraid you're not going to like it."

Anne turned the page to find a boxed sidebar story finishing the article. The headline read HAS JOSIAH RETURNED IN HIS GREAT-GRANDSON?

> Josiah Breck scandalized the territory in the nineteenth century by living with an Indian squaw but never marrying her, even after their son was born. His descendant seems to be following in his footsteps by living with a woman, not an Indian but an artist, outside of the traditional bonds of marriage.
>
> The proud and beautiful Anne Keene makes it very clear to visitors that she is not Mrs. Breck. Yet, the look in her eyes, the way she speaks, and the way she defers to one and only one man leave no question as to her relationship with the master of the house.

An angry flush rose to Anne's cheeks, but she continued to read.

> That is not the only way in which Jeremy Breck emulates his great-grandfather. He is a man of charismatic presence, dominating any room he enters. When Jeremy stands near the portrait of Josiah, it is easy to see the bond between generations.

The article went on to enumerate ways in which Jeremy resembled Josiah, not only in appearance but in behavior. Anne read without really absorbing anything—she was too shocked at Michael Barnes's description of herself.

"Calm down," Jeremy said gently. "You look as if you're about to start breaking things. It isn't as bad as it sounds when you read through it quickly, and it isn't as if he called you a harlot. These are the 1980s, Anne. Lots of people live together, and most people don't think anything about it."

"That's one thing. But to have it written up in a national magazine. Whatever happened to privacy?"

"Anne, don't worry about it. Nobody cares about that sort of thing."

"*I* do," Anne snapped, feeling suddenly confused. She had never felt any guilt or remorse about her relationship with Jeremy in the past months; living with him had been the most natural thing in the world. But that was different from having it discussed in a national magaine.

"You could have fooled me as recently as last night," Jeremy replied. There was an edge of anger in his voice, but he sounded chiefly puzzled.

"I can't stay here any longer," Anne said firmly. "I'll start moving my things this afternoon. The weather is warming up and my shop will be fine. I would have had to move back to open it in a few weeks anyway."

"Anne, I can't believe you're being such a child about this. So what if people know we're sleeping together?"

Anne's temper finally got the better of her for the first time in months. "I'm *not* about to be the sideshow entertainment at the Paradise Inn. You may not care about what people think of you, but I do. I can't pretend that the social conventions of the rest of the world just don't exist."

"*Anne* Anne, come back here and talk about this like an adult," Jeremy shouted after her as she ran from the room.

But Anne wasn't listening. She ran blindly up the stairs and into her room, then furiously started throwing clothes in her suitcase. Jeremy came to the door but didn't step inside.

"I don't understand your attitude," he said. "If we could talk about it—"

"If you want to talk to me, come to my shop after I've moved back there," Anne replied without turning to face him. She didn't dare look him in the eye. That was the trap; she knew what his eyes could do to her.

"All right. If this is what you want," Jeremy said quietly. "I'll take your worktable down this afternoon." When Anne turned to face the door, Jeremy was gone.

Not that she could have seen him clearly if he had been there. Her vision was blurred with tears. If only she could have seen the truth months ago, she thought bitterly. But that was the way of things; sometimes you got too close to a situation to see it clearly. She had spent the last four months mooning like a love-sick teenager over Jeremy Breck, never even suspecting the truth. It took an outsider like Michael Barnes to see the way things really were. Now Anne knew why Jeremy wanted her to live with him. He'd made plans for her from the very start—from the moment he walked into her shop that first night. She was perfect for him; an artist was exactly the kind of woman he wanted for his mistress. It all fit so nicely into the image he wanted to project of being the reincarnation of Josiah Breck. Just bohemian enough to create the right atmosphere, yet practical enough to be a help to him.

Of course, Jeremy wasn't the reincarnation of Josiah Breck. Josiah was a hard-headed, down-to-earth, hardworking lumberman who had parlayed his charisma and good luck into an empire. Jeremy was a well-educated, city-bred businessman who was trying to use his charm, wits, and big-money backing to build his own empire, but he needed props to convince people of his bond to Josiah. And I was the most important piece of set dressing, Anne thought bitterly.

After packing her belongings, Anne made three trips in the Volkswagen to move them all to her shop, and she didn't see Jeremy again. He must have been trying to stay out of her way, because when she arrived at her shop the third time, her worktable was already there. He had brought it between her trips, taking care that they didn't meet in the drive or at the door.

The remainder of the afternoon and evening were spent putting away her belongings and cleaning up. Everything was covered with a thin layer of dust that clung stubbornly as she wiped furiously with a dust rag.

The glass pieces she had left behind were in dismal condition, very dull and dusty. Anne knew it would take the better part of a week to polish each piece individually so it would be attractive to customers again.

Customers, she thought, happy to grasp any optimistic thought. Spring was just around the corner and soon there would be tourists again—more tourists than ever before, thanks to Jeremy, the Paradise Inn, and *American Vacation* magazine. There was hope. With the money she had from building the window, Anne could easily make it through this season, which promised to be better than the one before.

She slept fitfully that night. Her shop was a strange place now and Anne kept waking up and staring around the room in the dim light, wondering where she was. She would reach out, only to find she was alone, then memories would wash over her and she'd sink back to cry more tears into her pillow and drift into yet another bout of uneasy sleep. When she woke the next morning her sheets and blankets were twisted into tangled ropes and her bare arms were uncomfortably cold in the unheated room.

Anne got up and went to start a fire in her stove, even though she was stiff and bleary-eyed, and felt as if she hadn't slept at all. When she looked in the mirror, she was distressed by the puffy face and red eyes that looked back at her. She went into the bathroom to wash her face furiously, as if she could scrub off the marks of anguish. When she finished, her skin was pink from scrubbing, but the face that looked back at her still looked lost and hopeless.

"*Stop* it," she said angrily at the mirror. "Pull yourself together. You're lucky you found out in time."

There was still plenty of cleaning to be done around the shop, especially in the salesroom after four months of standing idle. Anne worked intensely through the morning, hardly looking up from the polishing cloth and sun catchers as she carefully removed the film of dust from each piece of glass and polished it to a jewellike shine.

It was almost noon when she reached up to take down a piece over the sales counter and her eyes fell on the telephone. Looking straight at it jarred her back to the things she didn't want to think about. How strange, she thought. Jeremy must have been paying the bill every month while I was up there. She wondered why he had bothered. She'd had no use for the phone; it had just hung on the wall in her closed shop all winter.

"Well, it's got to go," she said out loud as she reached to pick it up and call the phone company. Before she finished dialing, however, it occurred to Anne that there was no reason to remove it. She could afford it now. True, Jeremy had put it there and it would always remind her of him, but wasn't she an adult who could live with an object that reminded her of something unpleasant? The phone would be convenient; not having one now would be foolish. When the operator answered, she requested that the billing be changed to her own name.

With that taken care of, Anne returned to her work. She polished glass throughout the balance of the day and went to bed with a headache from the eyestrain of doing one close task all day long.

Anne expected to hear from Jeremy at any time. The phone was going to ring, and he would be on the line begging her to reconsider. Or he was going to show up at her door with flowers and make his plea in person. It made sense; he had invested months in grooming her to play the part of his mistress and Anne was sure he wouldn't give up so easily.

But he didn't call and didn't appear. It was as if the past months had never existed. A week later, Anne ran into Mrs. Harkness in the grocery store in Paradise. As she saw the housekeeper pushing her cart through the produce section, Anne considered ducking down another aisle to avoid her, but Mrs. Harkness spotted her before she could move.

"Anne," she called out. It was too late to hide, so Anne put on a cheery smile and went over to say hello.

"Is everything all right at the house?" Anne asked politely.

"As well as can be expected. Mr. Breck is out of town. He packed up and went to Chicago right after you left. It feels kind of strange to keep house in an empty building. There's no one to clean up after."

"I know what you mean. That place is too big for one person."

"If you don't mind my asking, what got into you? Everything was fine one minute, then you went storming out of the house."

Anne cleared her throat and looked embarrassed.

"None of my business, eh? Well, you know me. I figure everything is my business. Shall I give you a call when Mr. Breck comes back? You could say you forgot something and come up to the house. I bet you could get everything straightened out."

"I didn't leave anything behind."

"So what? I'll come over to your place this afternoon and get something."

"Thanks anyway," Anne said uncomfortably. "Well, it was nice seeing you. I'd better be going."

"Anne, don't give me that. You don't have to run away from *me*. I'm still your friend, even if you're on the outs with Mr. Breck."

"I know," Anne said with a forced smile. "I didn't mean to hurt your feelings. I just don't feel very social right now. Why don't you come down to my shop sometime for a cup of coffee?"

Another week passed without a word from Jeremy. Anne decided that his indifference to her leaving only proved her worst suspicions. He didn't really care about her. She was just a convenient person to fit into his plans. She wondered if his trip to Chicago was somehow related to finding her replacement. She knew Jeremy Breck too well to think that he would do without a female companion for very long. His new lady would undoubtedly be more cooperative and pliable than she had been.

On Tuesday of the third week after she left the Breck house, when spring was doing its best to supersede winter and the air was damp and warm and the ground cold and muddy, there was a knock at her door and Anne opened it to find Jeremy standing on her front step. He was wearing a brown windbreaker and blue jeans, and Anne almost gasped when she saw him. Just the sight of him could still make her heart beat faster. The March wind ruffled his dark curls and his cheeks were a healthy red. Without an invitation he stepped inside and wiped the spring mud off his shoes on the door mat.

Anne stood dumbly watching him. She didn't know what to say.

"Some mail came for you at the house," he said in a flat voice.

"Thank you for bringing it down," Anne replied in the same tone. She had to struggle to control her voice.

Jeremy looked around the shop. "I see you've done a lot of cleaning."

"Amazing how dirty things can get even when no one is there to use them."

Jeremy unexpectedly stopped his wandering around the shop and faced Anne squarely. "I'd like you to consider coming back, Anne."

Anne was thrown off guard by the abrupt change of subject, but that was just like Jeremy. He knew all the tricks for disarming an opponent.

"It took you long enough to come and ask," Anne said angrily. "I suppose you couldn't find a replacement on such short notice?"

"Anne," Jeremy said evenly, "I have no idea what you're talking about. To tell the truth, I waited so that you'd have a chance to calm down, look at the situation objectively, and make up your mind about what you really want."

"What I really want is not to have your guests coming up here to gawk at Jeremy Breck's 'artist-mistress.'"

"I really don't think they will, but if that's all that is bothering you, we can get married."

A feeling of helplessness washed through Anne. She was suddenly revolted by Jeremy's seeming insensitivity. "Thanks a heap," she said sarcastically. "I realize that business marriages are part of your regular mode of operation, but you of all people should know that I'd like a little more than a working relationship with a husband."

"I don't understand what you're talking about."

"Don't you? Well, think about it a little, Jeremy. When I get married, it will be because I'm in love and I intend to spend the rest of my life with that man. I'm not going to make a convenient arrangement and break it off when I'm ready to try something else."

Jeremy's face clouded with anger. "If you think I'm offering you a convenient arrangement, you're sadly mistaken. I've lived that kind of life and believe me it's not worth the effort. I love you, Anne. Why is that so difficult for you to believe? What does it take to get through to you?"

"What does it take?" Anne replied with difficulty. Her throat was tightening and uncalled-for tears threatened to spill out of her eyes. "I'd like to see you do just one thing that wasn't for the good of your precious Paradise Inn. Well, you have your window—I've made my contribution—so why don't you go away and leave me alone."

"Ah, I see. You really believe I've been using you, don't you? But what about you? Can you say that you weren't using me, or that the only reason you stayed on after your work was done was because this place is hard to heat? Can you honestly say that the only thing that brought you to my house was the window?"

Anne pressed her lips together and didn't answer. Any word she tried to say now would come out only as a sob.

"I won't wait forever, Anne," he said angrily. "You've been living in my house, sharing my bed—sharing everything I own and everything I've planned. Am I being unreasonable to ask for something from you in return? Am I a fool for wanting you to make some kind of commitment? You needed time to make up your own mind and I've given you all the time and patience I've got. I can't wait a lifetime for you to grow up. So this is it. All you have to do is say that you don't love me, that all you really care about is your business, and I'll go away and never bother you again."

Anne breathed deeply, trying to find her voice within the emotional anguish she felt. He was lying—he had to be. Jeremy would do anything, say anything, to get what he wanted. He had used money to lure her in the beginning and later he had used her own passionate nature to hold her. She had to ignore the part of her that was saying "Who cares why he wants you?" and let the rational part of her mind answer.

She forced her lips to move and form the words. "I don't love you. Your help has made all the difference to my business, Jeremy, and I'll always be grateful to you for that." She stared down at the floor to avoid looking into the powerful eyes that could strip away her pretense and force her to tell the truth.

"I won't ask you again, Anne," Jeremy replied quietly. "I just want you to know that I feel sorry for you. You once told me that you wanted independence, but you're never going to get it this way. You can never really be independent until you can make a commitment without leaving yourself a way out. Playing it safe is just another kind of bondage. And going it alone is a sterile kind of life."

Anne turned away, wishing he would leave.

"Your mail," he said, setting down the packet of letters on the counter. "If I read return addresses correctly, you're going to be having all the business success you can use. Some of those letters are from construction companies. They're probably invitations to bid on window jobs."

"What?" Anne said incredulously, picking up the mail. "How did they hear about me?"

"The magazine article. *American Vacation* has a large readership. You are now a well-known glass artist. I hope that makes you happy, Anne. I hope it's a good enough substitute for having a real life." He said the last words without sarcasm. It was almost a benediction.

Anne concentrated on the letters in her hands and didn't look up until she heard the door close behind Jeremy. She set the letters back on the counter without a second thought as the pent-up emotions burst forth and the tears streamed unchecked down her cheeks.

Chapter Eleven

Anne went about the routine of her life like a machine for the next week. She couldn't banish the terrible feeling of loss that followed her like a shadow, so she made up her mind not to feel anything. She got up in the morning, dressed, ate a light meal, and went about her shop like a ghost—lighting on a task but never attacking it with any conviction, then moving on to toy with something else. The nights were worse. Anne thought she would get used to sleeping alone again, having done it all her life before she met Jeremy, but each night was like the one before. She tossed and turned, waking again and again in the darkness to reach out for the warm, solid form that wasn't there.

She read the letters Jeremy had brought. Just as he had said, they were invitations to bid on various projects. One was from a firm building a new city hall in Tiffin, Ohio; they wanted the city crest rendered in stained glass for the lobby. Another was from the First Methodist Church of Fort Wayne, Indiana. The third was for a huge window, thirty feet high by forty feet wide, in a new Catholic church in Minneapolis, Minnesota. The contractor for that job offered to supply a crew to help with the heavy work if she would design and supervise the window.

Anne felt little enthusiasm for any of the offers, but she sifted through them and evaluated them just the same. She knew she had to get something started in

her life to take the place of what she had lost. She was
surprised at the distances the offers came from. To
accept any of them, she would have to travel far from
Paradise.

After much deliberation she answered the offer from
Minneapolis. It was by far the largest of the jobs, and
after doing the windows in Jeremy's house, she felt
that she needed a bigger challenge; she needed a job
that would require so much of her that she would
forget everything else.

As the crocuses poked little green spears out of the
thawing ground and buds swelled on the trees, Anne
worked feverishly, calculating a bid for the Minneapolis job. She took no notice of the shy hints of green
that appeared in the woods and along the edges of the
highway. She didn't bother to open her windows when
the weather turned warm and the air turned sweet
with spring flowers. She cursed the mud that col-
lected on the soles of her shoes on those rare occasions
when she went outside, but failed to notice the bloom-
ing daffodils and grape hyacinths.

Had people who knew her been around, they would
have been distressed by her apathy toward everything
that was happening around her and the way she dressed
without any attention to her appearance. But no one
was around. She went into town once a week to shop
for groceries and avoided all contact with people the
rest of the time.

But Anne didn't mind the isolation. She savored
her loneliness. When no one was around, she would
tell herself that no one mattered to her and the Minneapolis job was the most important thing that had ever
come into her life. She looked to the future with grim
determination, planning her life as a successful and
sought-after artist.

She submitted her bid for the Minneapolis job, and
received word by telephone only a few days later that

she had won the contract. The contractor wanted the window to be under way before the end of April, so she prepared to go to Minnesota. The glass she ordered would be delivered to the construction site and she'd live in a nearby hotel while she worked. Anne packed a suitcase with her work clothes and tools, and made a reservation to fly to Minneapolis on April 15.

She was preparing to close her shop and leave when she remembered that this was the day Jeremy had chosen to open the Paradise Inn. Anne would be leaving Paradise just as the Paradise Inn began its new life. When she arrived at the airport, she would very likely pass the first guests.

Before leaving the shop, she phoned the airport in Newberry to confirm her flight, and was distressed when she learned that her plane would be delayed for several hours by an equipment breakdown. Anne hung up the phone, wondering what she was going to do with herself for half a day. She had everything in the shop put away or covered with cloth to keep away dust, and she didn't want to hang around. After a moment's thought she loaded the suitcase in her car and drove into town to wander around while she waited.

She had dressed for the flight in a light gray linen suit and pink silk blouse. Her hair had grown longer in the year she had been in Paradise, so she'd abandoned her more casual hairstyle and pinned her blond curls into a neat French twist.

As she walked down Main Street, window-shopping to kill time, Anne became aware of the appreciative smiles she was drawing from the men she met on the street. At first she returned each look with an icy stare, but after a while the pleasant spring weather began to lift her spirits and she started to enjoy herself, smiling back, even stopping to say hello to a few people she recognized. She hadn't felt this good for weeks. She opened her senses to her surroundings and felt her spirits renewed just as the world was being renewed by springtime.

It was an absolutely perfect spring day. The sun was shining brightly on the clean streets and storefronts. Flowers bloomed in the flower boxes and birdsong blended with the street sounds. Anne walked down to the waterfront and looked out over the deep blue waters of Lake Superior. Fishing boats dotted the horizon while gulls wheeled overhead. The pungent odor of smoked fish blended with the perfume of spring and the sharp, clean smell of the lake water. With a pang of regret, Anne realized that from this day on, she would return to Paradise only to leave again. Her work was going to take her far from this place that she loved so much. There was only so much work for a stained-glass artist here; the glass she could sell to tourists was insignificant when compared to the work she could do elsewhere.

Had Jeremy known what he was starting when he ordered that window? Of course not. But now her business was taking on a life of its own, to go beyond her control and become something that she would have to serve, rather than the thing that would serve her, as she had always imagined. Anne was slightly uncomfortable with that thought. There was something else—some idea she was missing that would complete the picture.

She turned away from the waterfront and walked back toward the center of town. On the way, she passed the Paradise Public Library and paused. This was the library that Florence Breck had started.

It was a small white frame building with a sign proclaiming its function on the front lawn. Irises and tulips bloomed in the well-tended flowerbeds and the white clapboard building fairly sparkled in the spring sunshine. In her year of living near Paradise, Anne had never gone inside the library. Today, however, would be different. Anne turned up the walk and went inside to look for a diversion until it was time to leave for the airport.

Inside, the library was calming in its stillness and sense of order. The odor of old books filled the air, but it was far from stuffy. Anne felt that she had walked into a place where the past was alive and well.

"May I help you?" Anne started and spun around to face the librarian. She hadn't noticed the woman working behind the desk when she walked in. She was pleasant-looking, with short, steel-gray hair and sparkling blue eyes. Anne guessed that she was about the same age as Mrs. Harkness.

"Not really," Anne said with a smile. "I just came in to browse a little."

"Aren't you Anne Keene?" the librarian asked.

"Yes, I am," Anne replied. "But I don't believe we've met. Or if we have, I'm afraid I've forgotten your name."

"I'm Nettie Johnson. And, no, we've never met. I saw your picture in *American Vacation* magazine. You live up at the old house with Mr. Breck, don't you?"

Anne started to correct the woman's misconception but decided against calling attention to the subject. It would be better just to let it drop, she thought. She smiled uncomfortably. "That magazine article certainly gets around, doesn't it?" she replied.

"Having Paradise featured in a national magazine doesn't happen often," Nettie said with a proud smile. "It was a fine day when Mr. Breck came back to Paradise. Things are really going to take off around here."

"Well, I think I'll just find a book and sit down to read for a while," Anne said. "It was nice meeting you."

"What would you like? A mystery? If you have only a short time, maybe you'd like a collection of short stories?"

Anne knew that the librarian was only trying to be polite and helpful, but she really wanted to get away from the woman. Suddenly she wanted to be alone again. The mention of Jeremy had thrown her feelings into turmoil and she wanted some solitude to pull herself together.

"I'm not really sure what I want. I'll just browse and see what catches my eye."

"Wait. I have just the thing for you. I wouldn't get this out for just anybody, but since you're so close to Mr. Breck, I just know you'll find this fascinating."

The librarian motioned to Anne to follow her and led the way to a small room off the main section. A machine for reading microfilm occupied most of the worktable in the center of the room and one wall was given over to microfilm storage cabinets. The rest of the room was filled with the periodicals collection—bookshelves stacked with carefully catalogued magazines. One shelf, however, was filled with very old books and some obviously hand-bound volumes. The librarian reached up and gently took down one of the books.

"This is the historical collection," she said proudly as she set the book down on the table. "These books aren't for general circulation. They wouldn't last long if we let everybody handle them, but I think I can trust you to be careful."

"What is it?" Anne asked, looking at the blank cover of the book.

"The history of the Breck family. Jeremy Breck's mother compiled it. She privately published a few dozen copies and most of them went to family members. We feel very fortunate in having one here. Even though she never wrote professionally, Mrs. Breck was really a very good writer. This family history reads like a novel." The librarian smiled and carefully opened the cover of the book. "I think it's one of the most fascinating books we have, but maybe you've already seen it at the house."

"No, I haven't," Anne replied. She was suddenly very curious about the book. Jeremy had never mentioned it and she almost felt she was eavesdropping. Anne no longer had any connection with the Breck family, and their history was really none of her concern. But she had an itch to see what Jeremy's mother had written. Jeremy had mentioned that she had wanted to be a writer.

Anne sat down at the table and examined the title page: *The Life and Fortunes of the Breck Family,* by Marjorie Campbell Breck.

"When you're finished, just leave it out on the table," the librarian said. "I'll put it back later." She left Anne alone, closing the door behind her.

Anne scanned the first chapter with only minor interest. Marjorie had done a thorough genealogical study, tracing the Breck family back to Holland and England. Anne's interest picked up when she reached the part where Josiah's father came from England to a small farm in Connecticut. The War of 1812 drove the Brecks from their land and the family moved to northern Ohio. Josiah was born in Amsden Corners, Ohio, while his father was working as a farmhand in the area.

The second chapter began as Josiah left home at the age of nineteen to seek his fortune as a lumberjack in the still-wild Upper Penninsula of Michigan.

I think it only proper at this time to set straight a rather deceptive story about my grandmother-in-law, Dominique Talltrees. For reasons known only to them, the men of this family have been perpet-

uating a falsehood about this noble woman. Though
she died long before I was born, I feel a special
kinship to Dominique. She was as much a lady as
any woman born in the civilized houses of Europe.
Though she was a full-blooded Indian, the term
"squaw" does not seem to fit her.

The story that Josiah purchased her and kept
Dominique as a woman of low morals apparently
started as a private joke between Josiah and his
common-law wife. The story has now been perpet-
uated to such an extent that it is generally accepted as truth. The true account that follows
was told to me by Florence Breck, who, although
she was often in conflict with her mother-in-law
during the years they shared the house, respected
Dominique very much.

Anne read on with greater interest. Like Marjorie,
she felt a special attachment to Dominique.

Dominique was the daughter of an Ojibwa chief.
Her father had been converted to Catholicism by
French missionaries as a young man, discarding
his Indian name to be christened Jacques Talltrees
and naming his daughter after St. Dominic. Although Jacques was a devout Christian, he never
really grasped many of the subtleties of his new
faith. When the English settlers, most of whom
were Protestants, came to his area, he believed
them to be followers of a different religion al-
together and even believed that his Catholic God
was in conflict with theirs. He was a relentless
proselytizer and was often seen exhorting a new
settler to give up his satanic ways and come to
the True Faith.

Jacques Talltrees was at first tolerated by the
white men. He was, after all, a Christian and

therefore considered better than most heathen savages. In the long run, however, he was considered a nuisance. He often had to be escorted back to the reservation by the military authorities, if only for his own safety.

Dominique was frequently seen in the lumber camps. She helped support her family by doing laundry and mending for the men there. She had been well educated by the French priests and could read and write in both French and English. She was probably better educated than most of the white men she worked for, but as an Indian, she was allowed to do nothing but menial labor.

Once, when Reverend Jacques, as he was sarcastically called by the lumbermen, had been making a particularly bad nuisance of himself, a group of drunken soldiers took it upon themselves to teach the old Indian a lesson—through his young daughter, Dominique. It was this group, harassing Dominique, and probably planning much worse sport, that Josiah came upon on his way back to the camp.

Josiah pushed his way into the group and told them to leave the girl alone, but they laughed at him and called him a squaw lover. There were far too many of them for Josiah to take on by himself, though he was known as quite a brawler, so he looked for another method to rescue the camp's laundry girl. He was on his way back to the camp from the trading post, where he had purchased several bottles of whiskey for a friend—Josiah was not a drinking man himself. He had very little money, having spent most of that month's wages for the supplies he had packed on his mule, so he went up to the soldier who seemed to be the ringleader and offered him all the money he had on him to leave the girl alone. When the bully saw how little Josiah had, he only laughed. Desperately, Josiah offered the whiskey he had on the pack mule. The man was interested now but still not convinced. In the end, Dominique's safety cost Josiah all his money, the whiskey, the mule, and all the supplies. It was a steep price to pay for the safety of a girl he barely knew, but Josiah was a principled man and couldn't simply walk away and leave Dominique with the drunken soldiers.

Josiah told Dominique to go back to the reservation and stay there for several weeks until things cooled down, but Dominique refused to go. She followed him back to the lumber camp and insisted upon working for him, giving him all her laundry wages, until the money he had spent to save her was repaid. Not long after, Josiah went to Dominique's father and asked for her hand in marriage.

Jacques would not consent to the union. Josiah was a Protestant, and Jacques would allow his daughter to marry only a Catholic; Protestants were no better than heathen in his eyes. Dominique would not go against her father's wishes and marry Josiah without his consent. However, typical to Jacques' imperfect understanding of Christianity, he didn't mind if Dominique lived with a Protestant; it was only the religious ceremony that he objected to.

While Jacques lived, Dominique wouldn't marry Josiah, and the old man lived a long time. Dominique and Josiah had been living together for more than twenty-five years when he died. I can't truly say why they never married after that, except that they probably thought it unnecessary.

Anne closed the book and paused to think about what she had just read. Jeremy had to know the truth;

surely he would have read his mother's book. Why had he told the same lie that everybody else believed?

"How I misunderstood you, Dominique, Anne said quietly. "I always thought you didn't have choices, but you had control of everything that happened in your life. You didn't wait for someone to tell you what you ought to do—you made up your mind about what was right and then did it. And since you knew you were right, you didn't care what anybody else thought. You chose to love and serve Josiah. The only hold he had on you was that love. How could I have been so stupid? I've spent my life waiting for someone to hand me my independence on a silver platter. I wanted somebody to tell me it was all right to do what I wanted, but I don't need anybody to tell me what's right. I already know. You weren't that stupid, were you, Dominique?"

The librarian poked her head in the door of the reference room. "Did you want something?" she asked. "I heard you say something."

"Uh, no. I was just talking to myself. I guess I was a bit distracted." She glanced at her watch and saw that it was time to leave if she was going to make it to the airport on time. "I'm finished now, if you want to put the book away." Anne got up and smiled at the librarian. "And thank you for showing it to me. You're absolutely right—it's fascinating."

Anne left the library and walked out into the warm spring sunshine. Her car was several blocks away and she started to hurry. She had very little time to spare if she was going to make her flight. But when she got into the driver's seat, Anne knew she was going to miss the plane; she didn't *want* to leave Paradise.

It was her decision. She didn't have to do windows all over the country if she didn't want to, and that had never been part of Anne's plan. The mere fact that she'd been invited to bid on the Minneapolis window didn't mean she was obligated to do it. She hadn't signed a contract yet. They were going to take care of the paperwork when she got there.

Anne started the engine and drove out of town on the road that led to her shop, but she passed Keene's Kraft Kabin without a second look. She knew where she was going and what she was going to do without thinking about it. She didn't have to make a plan. Anne was going to do what her heart told her was right, even if nobody in the world approved.

Turning up the drive to the Breck house, Anne stopped before she got within sight of the house and got out her suitcase. She opened it carefully and removed the small jewelry box she had packed. Inside was the necklace Jeremy had given her for Christmas.

There had been several times during the past few weeks when she had considered returning it to him, but something had always stopped her. It may have been because it was such a beautiful piece of jewelry, but more likely Anne hadn't returned it because the necklace was her last tie to the Breck family. In the months that she had lived in the house, she had come to love Josiah and Dominique, and even the haughty Florence, accepting them as if they were her own family. Then, when Jeremy seemed to slip out of her grasp, she had been loath to give up that last possession that linked her to them, and now she was glad she hadn't. She drew it carefully from the box and put it around her neck on top of her blouse.

With the necklace hanging prominently around her neck, Anne got back into the car and drove up to the house. A new lawn was sprouting where the old weeds had been removed last fall, the freshly painted trim shone cleanly in the midday spring sun, and the red brick seemed brighter than she had ever seen it. Anne took her suitcase out of the car and carried it to the front door.

She let herself in and looked around the entry hall with pleasure. It was like coming home. She could see that Jeremy had gone to great lengths to make everything perfect for the opening day. A vase of cut flowers stood on the hall table under the mirror and everything had been cleaned and polished. Anne stepped into the office and set down her suitcase to sign the guest register. When she turned back, she found Jeremy standing in the door. His face betrayed nothing. It might have been carved in granite as he neither smiled nor frowned. He just looked at her.

For a moment Anne's resolve weakened. Not long ago, in her shop, he had said that their relationship was over. She had hoped to see some sign in him that he wanted her to come back, but as soon as she thought of it, she steeled herself to go through with her plan. She didn't need his permission to love him. It was all up to her now.

"I was going to catch a flight out of here today," Anne said to Jeremy's stony countenance, "but I missed it. I've got my shop closed down and I need a room for the night." She spoke confidently, as if her presence here was the most natural thing in the world.

"The motel in Paradise is cheaper and probably more convenient for a brief stay," Jeremy said flatly.

"I may have to stay for a while. I'm sure this is more comfortable than any motel," Anne replied.

"I see. How long do you think you'll be staying?"

"I don't know. It could be a long time before there's a flight out of here that goes to anyplace I want to go." Anne said these last words in a steady voice, looking Jeremy straight in the eye. At first the corner of his mouth twitched a bit—almost hidden by his mustache. Then the corners of his eyes crinkled as his whole face broke into a wide smile. Anne smiled back as Jeremy started to chuckle.

Crossing the scant six feet that separated them,

Anne put her arms around Jeremy's neck. "I'm not looking for an invitation. I'm already here and you're going to have a hard time getting me to leave again," she said.

"You finally looked inside the locket," he said.

"What locket?" Anne said, puzzled.

"What locket? The locket you've got on, silly." He paused, looking at her in wonder. "You mean you haven't looked inside? You came to this decision on your own?"

"I had some good advice from a wise old Indian woman," Anne replied. She took the necklace in her hand and examined it carefully. For the first time she noticed the fine, almost invisible seam that separated the two halves, and she carefully opened it.

Inside was a miniature portrait of Josiah. But the inside of the lid held the great surprise.

Dominique and Josiah Breck, married June 13, 1876, Philadelphia, Anne read in tiny engraved letters. "*What?* But even your mother's book said they never got married."

"Ah, you've read Mother's book. Well, even she didn't know everything. Nobody knew. Not even Florence and Morton. I know only because I found that locket in Dominique's jewelry box."

"But why did you lie to me about it? You knew the truth. Why did you let me go on believing the story that everyone tells about them?"

"Why should it matter? I'm not Josiah or Josiah's reincarnation, and you're not Dominique. After I found the locket, I thought about it a lot, and I think they actually preferred people to believe that story because it protected their privacy. They got married shortly after old Jacques died, but they kept it to themselves because it wasn't anybody else's business. They weren't worried about what people thought of them—they loved each other. People could gossip all they wanted.

It didn't do them any harm. They had all they wanted in each other."

"But if it doesn't matter, why didn't you tell me the truth?" Anne insisted.

Jeremy raised an eyebrow and chuckled. "Still the same one-track mind. Maybe if I'd known it would make such a big difference to you, I would have told you," he said, suddenly serious.

"I've been foolish about a lot of things," Anne said sincerely. "I thought that you were trying to recreate Josiah's life in your own, and I drew all kinds of silly parallels between Josiah and Dominique and you and me. But since I never knew the truth about your great-grandparents, none of it made any sense. But that was the smallest of my follies. I almost let my business become another drudge job, like the one I left behind. I forgot that I was in charge and didn't have to do anything I didn't want to do. But my worst mistake was that I never said I loved you. I should have said it a long time ago, but I was afraid. I don't suppose it really does make any difference how your great-grandparents lived—to anybody but them, that is. And yet if I hadn't learned the truth about Dominique today, I might never have seen how foolish I've been. I love you, Jeremy Breck. And though I'll be happier if you love me, too, it doesn't really matter whether you do or not. You're stuck with me and it's going to take a lot more than a window in Minneapolis to get rid of me."

"I never want to get rid of you," Jeremy replied. His strong arms closed around her as their lips met, and Anne let herself soar in the ecstasy of this embrace that surpassed any that had ever come before. As her heart beat faster and passion took hold of her body, she gave herself over—without fear, without regret. All the questions, all the doubts, were gone.

"I don't care who thinks we're living together," she

whispered in his ear. "Because they'll be absolutely right."

"Don't be ridiculous," Jeremy replied. "You don't think I'm going to let you be so unencumbered that you can walk out of here anytime you want, do you? I tried that once already and you almost did it. That was my big mistake, Anne. If you're going to live here, you're going to have to marry me."

"What? A Breck imprisoned by social convention?"

"Let Josiah fly in the face of social propriety," Jeremy replied. "That was his privilege and it seemed to work well for him, but *I* want guarantees. I want to know that fifty years from now, you'll still be here loving me."

"What happened to all that talk about flying without a safety net?" Anne asked with delight. "What happened to 'Hanging back to be safe only keeps what you want out of your grasp'?"

"Flying without a safety net is fine, but some things are too precious to risk. Say you'll marry me, Anne. Say you'll love me forever, not just while it's convenient and comfortable."

"Forever isn't long enough," Anne said quietly, "but it should do for a start."

RAPTURE ROMANCE

**Provocative and sensual,
passionate and tender—
the magic and mystery of love
in all its many guises
Coming next month**

BOUNDLESS LOVE by Laurel Chandler. *"Andrea, your new boss, Quinn Avery, intends to destroy everything you've been working for."* The warning haunted her, even as his sensuous lips covered her with kisses. Was Quinn just using her to further his career? Andrea had to know the truth—even if it broke her heart . . .

WINTER'S PROMISE by Kasey Adams. A chance meeting brought psychologist Laurel Phillips and a handsome vagabond, Cass, together in a night of unforgettable ecstasy. But, despite their shared love, what future was there for a successful career woman and a rootless wanderer?

BELOVED STRANGER by Joan Wolf. A winter storm left them in each other's arms, shy Susan Morgan and Ricardo Montoya, baseball's hottest superstar. Even though their worlds were so far apart, Susan found her love had a chance—if she only had the strength to grasp it . . .

STARFIRE by Lisa St. John. Shane McBride was overwhelmed by Dirk Holland's enigmatic magnetism as he invaded her fantasies—and her willing body. But soon Shane found herself caught in the love-web of a man who wanted to keep all his possessions to himself . . .

TELL US YOUR OPINIONS AND RECEIVE A FREE COPY OF THE RAPTURE NEWSLETTER.

Thank you for filling out our questionnaire. Your response to the following questions will help us to bring you more and better books. In appreciation of your help we will send you a free copy of the Rapture Newsletter.

1. Book Title: _____

   Book # : _____   (5-7)

2. Using the scale below how would you rate this book on the following features? Please write in one rating from 0-10 for each feature in the spaces provided. Ignore bracketed numbers.

(Poor) 0 1 2 3 4 5 6 7 8 9 10 (Excellent)
                                    0-10 Rating

Overall Opinion of Book................. _____ (8)
Plot/Story............................ _____ (9)
Setting/Location...................... _____ (10)
Writing Style......................... _____ (11)
Dialogue.............................. _____ (12)
Love Scenes........................... _____ (13)
Character Development:
Heroine:.............................. _____ (14)
Hero:................................. _____ (15)
Romantic Scene on Front Cover......... _____ (16)
Back Cover Story Outline .... _____ (17)
First Page Excerpts................... _____ (18)

3. What is your: Education: Age: _____ (20-22)

   High School   (   )1   4 Yrs. College (   )3
   2 Yrs. College (   )2   Post Grad   (   )4 (23)

4. Print Name: _____

   Address: _____

   City: _____ State: _____ Zip: _____

   Phone # (   ) _____ (25)

Thank you for your time and effort. Please send to New American Library, Rapture Romance Research Department, 1633 Broadway, New York, NY 10019.

GET SIX RAPTURE ROMANCES EVERY MONTH FOR THE PRICE OF FIVE.

Subscribe to Rapture Romance and every month you'll get six new books for the price of five. That's an $11.70 value for just $9.75. We're so sure you'll love them, we'll give you 10 days to look them over at home. Then you can keep all six and pay for only five, or return the books and owe nothing.

To start you off, we'll send you four books absolutely FREE. "Apache Tears," "Love's Gilded Mask," "O'Hara's Woman," and "Love So Fearful." The total value of all four books is $7.80, but they're yours *free* even if you never buy another book.

So order Rapture Romances today. And prepare to meet a different breed of man.

YOUR FIRST 4 BOOKS ARE FREE!
JUST PHONE 1-800-228-1888*

(Or mail the coupon below)
*In Nebraska call 1-800-642-8788

- -

Rapture Romance, P.O. Box 996, Greens Farms, CT 06436

Please send me the 4 Rapture Romances described in this ad FREE and without obligation. Unless you hear from me after I receive them, send me 6 NEW Rapture Romances to preview each month. I understand that you will bill me for only 5 of them at $1.95 each (a total of $9.75) with no shipping, handling or other charges. I always get one book FREE every month. There is no minimum number of books I must buy, and I can cancel at any time. The first 4 FREE books are mine to keep even if I never buy another book.

Name	(please print)
Address	City
State Zip	Signature (if under 18, parent or guardian must sign)

RR *RAPTURE ROMANCE*

This offer, limited to one per household and not valid to present subscribers, expires June 30, 1984. Prices subject to change. Specific titles subject to availability. Allow a minimum of 4 weeks for delivery.

RAPTURE ROMANCE

**Provocative and sensual,
passionate and tender—
the magic and mystery of love
in all its many guises
New Titles Available Now**

*Price is $2.25 in Canada

RAPTURE ROMANCE

*Provocative and sensual,
passionate and tender—
the magic and mystery of love
in all its many guises*

**Buy them at your local
bookstore or use coupon
on next page for ordering.**

RAPTURE ROMANCE

Provocative and sensual, passionate and tender— the magic and mystery of love in all its many guises

RAPTURE ROMANCE

Provocative and sensual,
passionate and tender—
the magic and mystery of love
in all its many guises

Buy them at your local

bookstore or use coupon

on next page for ordering.